**'If you're af
you have to d
loosened his already relaxed grip.**

Something—a wild spark of defiance—kept Hani still. A basic female instinct, honed by her past experiences, told her she had nothing to fear from Kelt.

'I'm not afraid of you.'

Kelt's expression altered fractionally; the glittering steel-blue of his gaze raked her face.

Hani held her breath when his mouth curved in a tight, humourless smile.

'Good.'

And then he bent his head the last few inches and at last she felt his mouth on hers, gentle and without passion, as though he was testing her.

The warnings buzzing through her brain disappeared in a flood of arousal. Kelt tasted of sinful pleasure, of erotic excitement, of smouldering sexuality focused completely on her and the kiss they were exchanging—a kiss she'd never forget.

**Robyn Donald** can't remember not being able to read, and will be eternally grateful to the local farmers who carefully avoided her on a dusty country road as she read her way to and from school, transported to places and times far away from her small village in Northland, New Zealand. Growing up fed her habit; as well as training as a teacher, marrying and raising two children, she discovered the delights of romances and read them voraciously, especially enjoying the ones written by New Zealand writers. So much so that one day she decided to write one herself. Writing soon grew to be as much of a delight as reading—although infinitely more challenging—and when eventually her first book was accepted by Mills & Boon® she felt she'd arrived home. She still lives in a small town in Northland, with her family close by, using the landscape as a setting for much of her work. Her life is enriched by the friends she's made among writers and readers, and complicated by a determined Corgi called Buster, who is convinced that blackbirds are evil entities. Her greatest hobby is still reading, with travelling a very close second.

**Recent titles by the same author:**

THE MEDITERRANEAN PRINCE'S CAPTIVE VIRGIN
HIS MAJESTY'S MISTRESS
VIRGIN BOUGHT AND PAID FOR
INNOCENT MISTRESS, ROYAL WIFE
THE RICH MAN'S BLACKMAILED MISTRESS

# RICH, RUTHLESS AND SECRETLY ROYAL

BY
ROBYN DONALD

MILLS & BOON

*Pure reading pleasure*™

**DID YOU PURCHASE THIS BOOK WITHOUT A COVER?**

If you did, you should be aware it is **stolen property** as it was reported *unsold and destroyed* by a retailer. Neither the author nor the publisher has received any payment for this book.

All the characters in this book have no existence outside the imagination of the author, and have no relation whatsoever to anyone bearing the same name or names. They are not even distantly inspired by any individual known or unknown to the author, and all the incidents are pure invention.

All Rights Reserved including the right of reproduction in whole or in part in any form. This edition is published by arrangement with Harlequin Enterprises II BV/S.à.r.l. The text of this publication or any part thereof may not be reproduced or transmitted in any form or by any means, electronic or mechanical, including photocopying, recording, storage in an information retrieval system, or otherwise, without the written permission of the publisher.

This book is sold subject to the condition that it shall not, by way of trade or otherwise, be lent, resold, hired out or otherwise circulated without the prior consent of the publisher in any form of binding or cover other than that in which it is published and without a similar condition including this condition being imposed on the subsequent purchaser.

® and TM are trademarks owned and used by the trademark owner and/or its licensee. Trademarks marked with ® are registered with the United Kingdom Patent Office and/or the Office for Harmonisation in the Internal Market and in other countries.

First published in Great Britain 2009
Harlequin Mills & Boon Limited,
Eton House, 18-24 Paradise Road, Richmond, Surrey TW9 1SR

© Robyn Donald 2009

ISBN: 978 0 263 87428 0

Set in Times Roman 10½ on 12¼ pt
01-0909-49567

Printed and bound in Spain
by Litografia Rosés, S.A., Barcelona

# RICH, RUTHLESS AND SECRETLY ROYAL

# CHAPTER ONE

DRUMS pounded out into the sticky tropical night, their vigorous beat almost drowning out the guitars. Her smile tinged with strain, Hani Court surveyed the laughing, singing crowd from her vantage point at the other end of the ceremonial area.

The village people had thrown themselves into the celebrations with typical Polynesian gusto, the occasion their way of thanking the group of New Zealand engineering students who'd fixed and upgraded their derelict water system.

First there had been feasting, and now they were dancing. A teacher at the local school, Hani wasn't expected to join them.

Instead, watching the whirling, colourful patterns the dancers made, she resisted aching, nostalgic memories of Moraze, her distant homeland. There, beneath a tropical moon every bit as huge and silver as this one, men and women danced the *sanga*, an erotic expression of desire, without ever touching.

Here, half a world away on Tukuulu, the dancing was purely Polynesian but it shared the graceful hand movements and lithe sensuality of the *sanga*.

Six years ago Hani had accepted that she'd never dance the *sanga* again, never laugh with her brother Rafiq, never ride a horse across the wild, grassy plains of Moraze. Never hear her people cheer their ruler and his sister, the girl they'd called their little princess.

Never feel desire again…

Unfortunately acceptance didn't mean resignation. Pierced by longing for everything her stupidity had thrown away, she glanced around. She wasn't on duty, and no one would miss her if she sneaked back to her house in the teachers' compound.

A prickle of unease scudded down her spine. She drew in a breath, her stomach dropping into freefall when her eyes met a steel-blue scrutiny.

Transfixed, she blinked. He was taller than anyone else and the stranger's broad shoulders emphasised his height; hard, honed features provided a strong framework for a starkly handsome face. But what made him stand out in the exuberant crowd was his formidable confidence and the forceful authority that gave him an uncompromising air of command.

Every sense on full alert, Hani froze. Who was he? And why did he watch her so intently?

Quelling an instinctive urge to run, she felt her eyes widen as he walked towards her. Her tentative gaze clashed with a narrowed gleaming gaze, and a half-smile curved his hard, beautifully cut mouth. Colour swept up through her skin when she recognised the source of his interest.

Sexual appraisal.

OK, she could deal with that. But her relief was rapidly followed by shock at her body's tumultuous—and entirely unwelcome—response.

Never—not even the first time she'd met Felipe—had she experienced anything like the surge of molten sensation in every cell as the stranger came nearer, moving through the crowd with a silent, lethal grace. Her skin tightened, the tiny hairs lifting as though she expected an attack.

Warned by that secret clamour, she stiffened bones that showed a disconcerting tendency to soften and commanded her erratic heart to calm down.

*Cool it!* she told herself. He probably just wants a dance. Followed by a mild flirtation to while away the evening?

That thought produced an even faster pulse rate, pushing it up to fever pitch.

Perhaps he thought she was a local; although she was taller than most of the islanders her black hair and softly golden skin blended in well enough.

He stopped beside her. Bewildered and shocked, Hani felt his smile right down to her toes; it sizzled with a sexual charisma that emphasised the aura of controlled power emanating from him. With a jolt of foreboding she realised he was being eyed covertly or openly by most of the women within eyeshot.

Antagonism flared inside her. Here was a man who took his powerful masculine attraction for granted.

*Just like Felipe.*

But it was unfair to load him with Felipe's sins...

He said in a voice that made each word clear in spite of the background noise, 'How do you do? I'm Kelt Gillan.'

Struggling to dampen down her wildfire response, Hani smiled distantly, but she couldn't ignore the greeting or the fact that he obviously thought a handshake would be the next step.

Nor could she pretend not to feel the scorching along her cheekbones when she looked up and found his gaze on her mouth. Hot little shivers ran through her at that gaze—darkly intent, too perceptive.

'Hannah Court,' she said, hoping the aloof note in her voice would frighten him off.

Of course, he didn't scare easily. One black brow lifted.

Reluctantly she extended her hand, and his fingers closed around hers.

Hani flinched.

'Did I hurt you?' he demanded, frowning.

'No, no, not at all.' He had, in fact, judged to a nicety exactly how much strength to exert. Fumbling for a reason she could give him at her involuntary reaction, she hurried on, 'Just—I think someone walked over my grave.'

It took every shred of her fragile control not to snatch back her hand. His fingers were warm and strong—the hand of a person who worked hard.

But it wasn't his calluses that sent another bolt of sensation through her, so fiercely intense it numbed her brain and left her with nothing to say.

Rescue came from the band; abruptly, the drums and music fell silent. The dancers stopped and turned to the back of the dance floor.

The stranger looked over her head, his eyes narrowing as Hani found enough voice to warn, 'The elders have arrived. It's polite to be quiet.'

He didn't look like someone who'd care about the rituals of Polynesian society, but after a quick nod he watched the aristocratic council of men and women who ruled Tukuulu file past.

Hani dragged in a deep breath. The leaders would produce their best oratory to thank the group of students, and on Tukuulu it was an insult to leave while they spoke. So although she was stuck beside this man for some time, at least she wouldn't have to talk to him.

She'd have time to subdue the wild confusion attacking her. And then she'd think up some innocuous conversation. Not that she cared if he assumed she was a halfwit, she decided defiantly.

Willing herself to keep her gaze on the elders as they

positioned themselves in front of the crowd, she wondered where he'd come from and what he was doing here. Although his height and those burnished eyes, the cold blue of the sheen on steel, hinted at a northern-European heritage, his olive skin spoke of the Mediterranean.

Perhaps he was Australian, or from New Zealand, although she couldn't recall an accent.

As for what he was doing here—well, right next door was the big nickel mine, Tukuulu's only industry, so possibly he had something to do with that.

If so, Hani thought trenchantly, she'd try to persuade him that the mine company needed to accept some responsibility for the school that educated its workforce.

About half an hour into the speeches, Hani blinked, then closed her eyes against the light from the flaring torches.

*Not here, not now,* she prayed fervently. *Please!*

Cautiously she lifted her lashes, only to blink again as the flames splintered into jagged shards that stabbed into her brain. Heat gathered across her temples, while a dragging ache weighted her bones.

The fever had returned.

Don't panic—just stay upright. Once they finish you can go.

For almost two months—ever since the last bout—she'd been so sure she'd finally managed to shake off this wretched bug. Fear hollowed her stomach; the last time she'd been ill with it the principal had told her that another bout would mean some months spent recuperating in a more temperate climate.

But she had nowhere to go, and no money…

Acutely aware of the silent woman at his side, Kelt Crysander-Gillan concentrated on the speeches. Although he couldn't follow all the allusions, the Tukuuluan dialect was close enough to Maori for him to appreciate the sentiments and the aptness of the songs that followed each speaker.

Pity the council hadn't waited another ten minutes or so to arrive. Then he'd have had time to introduce himself properly to the woman with the intriguing face and the aloof, reserved air.

Looking down, he realised that she was sneaking a glance at him from beneath her lashes. When their eyes clashed she firmed her luscious mouth and looked away, providing him with an excellent view of her profile.

Kelt switched his gaze back to the orator, but that fine line of brow and nose, the determined little chin and the sleek gloss of exquisite skin stayed firmly lodged in his mind.

An islander? No. Not if her eyes were as green as they seemed to be. And although her silky fall of hair gleamed like jet, a quick glance around the room confirmed that not a single Tukuuluan shared the red highlights that gleamed across the dark sheen. A staff member? Probably. When he'd come in she'd been talking to one of the teachers.

He'd already ascertained she wore no rings.

More than an hour after they'd arrived, the elders finally sat down, giving the signal for the celebrations to continue. Immediately the hall exploded in chatter, swiftly over-whelmed by the renewed staccato thump of the drums.

And the woman beside him turned without speaking and walked away.

An ironic smile pulled at the corners of Kelt's mouth as he watched her. So much for the notorious Gillan pulling power! He couldn't recollect any other woman flinching when he shook hands.

His gaze sharpened when she appeared to stumble. She recovered herself and stood with bowed head and slumping shoulders.

Without volition, Kelt took two steps towards her, stopping when she straightened up and set off into the hot, dark embrace of the night.

But something was definitely wrong. She wasn't so much walking as lurching down the avenue of coconut palms, and while he watched she staggered again, managed another few steps, and then collapsed heavily against the trunk of the nearest tree.

Kelt set off after her, long legs eating up the distance. Once within earshot he demanded, 'Are you all right?'

Hani tried to straighten up when she heard the deep, cool, aloof voice—very male. Even in her distress she was pretty sure she knew who was speaking.

Weakly she said, 'Yes, thank you,' humiliated to realise she sounded drunk, the words slurred and uneven. She probably looked drunk too, huddled against the palm trunk.

'Can I get you anything?' This time he sounded curt and impatient.

'No.' Just go away, she pleaded silently.

'Drink or drugs?'

She longed for her usual crisp, no-nonsense tone when she responded, 'Neither.'

Instead the word dragged, fading into an indeterminate mutter. Closing her eyes, she tried to ignore him and concentrate on staying more or less upright.

He made a disgusted sound. 'Why don't I believe that?' Without waiting for an answer he picked her up as though she were a child and demanded, 'Where were you going?'

Fighting the debilitating desire to surrender and just let him look after her, she struggled to answer, finally dredging the words from her confused brain. 'Ahead—in house.'

He set off silently and smoothly, but by the time they

reached her door Hani's entire energy was focused on holding herself together long enough to take her medication before the fever crashed her into nightmare territory.

'Where's your key?'

'B-bag.' Her lips felt thick and unwieldy, and she said it again, but this time it was an inarticulate mutter. Dimly Hani heard him say something else, but the words jumbled around in her head.

Chills racked her shaking body as she whispered, 'Cold...so cold...'

Unconsciously she curled into the man who held her, striving to steal some of his warmth. Kelt's unruly body stiffened in automatic recognition and, swearing silently, he took the bag from her limp fingers. His arms tightened around her and he said, 'It's all right, I'll get you inside.'

She didn't appear to hear him. 'B-bedside,' she said, slurring the word.

She was shivering so hard he thought he heard her teeth chattering, yet she was on fire—so hot he could feel it through his clothes.

Kelt set her on her feet, holding her upright when she crumpled. He inserted the key and twisted it, picking her up again as soon as he had the door open. Once inside the small, sparsely furnished living room he found the light switch and flicked it on.

The woman in his arms stiffened, turning her head away from the single bulb. Her mouth came to rest against his heart, and through the fine cotton of his shirt he could feel the pressure of her lips against his skin.

Grimly, he tried to ignore his body's consuming response to the accidental kiss.

Guessing that the open door in the far wall probably led to

a bedroom, he strode towards it. Through the opening, one comprehensive glance took in an ancient institutional bed. A rickety lamp on the chest of drawers beside it seemed to be the only illumination.

He eased her down onto the coverlet, then switched on the lamp. Hannah Court gave a soft, sobbing sigh.

His first instinct was to call a doctor, but she opened her eyes—great eyes, darkly lashed, and yes, they were green.

Even glazed and unseeing, they were alluring.

'Pills.' Her voice was high and thin, and she frowned, her eyes enormous in her hectically flushed face. 'T-top drawer...'

Kelt's expression lightened a fraction when he saw a bottle of tablets; although he didn't recognise the name of the drug, the dose was clearly set out, headed rather quaintly For the Fever.

He said harshly, 'I'll get you some water.'

When he came back her eyes were closed again beneath her pleated brows. She'd turned away from the light, rucking up her skirt around her hips to reveal long, elegant legs. Setting his jaw against a swift stab of desire, Kelt jerked the fabric down to cover her.

'Hannah.' Deliberately he made his tone hard and commanding.

Still lost in that region of pain and fever, she didn't answer, but her lashes flickered. Kelt sat down on the side of the bed, shook out the right number of pills, and repeated her name. This time there was no response at all.

He laid the back of his hand against her forehead. Her skin was burning. Perhaps he should call a doctor instead of trying to get the medication inside her.

Medication first, he decided, then he'd get a doctor. 'Open your mouth, Hannah,' he ordered.

After a few seconds she obeyed. He put the pills onto her

tongue and said in the same peremptory tone, 'Here's the water. Drink up.'

Her body moved reflexively, but she did as she was told, greedily gulping down the water and swallowing the pills without any problems.

She even managed to sigh, 'OK—soon…'

Kelt eased her back onto the pillow and slipped the sandals from her slender, high-arched feet. She wasn't wearing tights, and her dress was loose enough to be comfortable.

To his surprise she made a soft protesting noise. One hand came up and groped for him, then fell onto the sheet, the long, elegant fingers loosening as another bout of shivering shook her slim body with such rigour that Kelt turned away and headed for the door. She needed help, and she needed it right now.

He'd almost got to the outer door when he heard a sound from the room behind him. Turning in mid-stride, Kelt made it back in half the time.

Hannah Court had fallen out of the bed, her slim body twisting as guttural little moans escaped through her clenched teeth.

What sort of fever took hold so quickly?

When he picked her up she immediately turned into him, unconsciously seeking—what? Comfort?

'Hannah, it's all right, I'll get a doctor for you as soon as I can,' he told her, softening and lowering his voice as though she were a child.

'Hani,' she whispered, dragging out the syllables.

Honey? A play on Hannah, a pet name perhaps? She certainly had skin like honey—even feverish it glowed, delicate and satin-smooth.

His arms tightened around her yielding body and he sat on

the side of the bed, surprised when the close embrace seemed to soothe her restlessness. Slowly, almost imperceptibly, the intense, dramatic shivers began to ease.

But when he went to lie her down she clutched weakly at him. 'Stay,' she mumbled so thickly it was difficult to make out the words. 'Stay. Please…Raf…' The word died away into an indeterminate mumble.

Rafe? A lover? Surprised and irritated by a fierce twist of what couldn't possibly be jealousy, Kelt said, 'It's all right, I won't let you go.'

That seemed to soothe her. She lay quiescent, her breathing becoming more regular.

Kelt looked down at her lovely face. His brother Gerd would laugh if he could see him now. This small, stark room couldn't have been a bigger contrast to the pomp of the ceremony he'd just attended in Carathia, when their grandmother had presented Gerd, their next ruler, to the people of the small, mountainous country on the Adriatic.

His brother had always known that one day he'd rule the Carathians, and Kelt had always been devoutly thankful the fishbowl existence of monarchy wasn't his fate. His mouth tightened. His own title of Prince Kelt, Duke of Vamili, had been confirmed too. And that should put an end to the grumblings of discontent amongst some of the less educated country people.

Last year their grandmother, the Grand Duchess of Carathia, had come down with a bout of pneumonia. She'd recovered, but she'd called Gerd back to Carathia, intent on sealing the succession of the exceedingly wealthy little country. The ceremonies had gone off magnificently with the world's royalty and many of its leaders in attendance.

As well as a flock of princesses.

With a cynical movement of his hard mouth, Kelt wondered if their grandmother would have any luck marrying her heir off to one.

He suspected not. Gerd might be constrained by centuries of tradition, but he'd choose his own wife.

And once that was done there would be children to seal the succession again. He frowned, thinking of a Carathian tradition that had complicated the existence of Carathian rulers. It had surfaced again—very inconveniently—just before the ceremonies. Someone had resurrected the ancient tale of the second child, the true chosen one, and in the mountains, where the people clung to past beliefs, a groundswell of rebellion was fomenting.

Fortunately he'd spent very little time in Carathia since his childhood, so his presence was no direct threat to Gerd's rule. But he didn't like what was coming in from his brother's informants and his own.

Instead of a simple case of someone fomenting mischief, the rumours were beginning to seem like the first step to a carefully organised plan to produce disorder in Carathia, and so gain control of over half of the world's most valuable mineral, one used extensively in electronics.

The woman in his arms sighed, and snuggled even closer, turning her face into his neck. Her skin no longer burned and she'd stopped shivering.

He registered that the distant throb of the music had stopped, and glanced at the clock on top of the chest of drawers. He'd been holding her for just over an hour. Whatever the medication was, it worked miraculously fast.

He responded with involuntary appreciation to her faint, drifting scent—erotic, arousing—and the feel of her, lax and quiescent against him as though after lovemaking. Cursing his unruly body and its instant reaction, he moved her so that he could see her face.

Yes, she was certainly on the mend. The flush had faded, and she was breathing normally.

A moment later beads of perspiration broke out through her skin. Astoundingly fast, the fine cotton of her dress was soaked, the fabric clinging like a second skin, highlighting the elegant bowl of her hips, the gentle swell of her breasts, the vulnerable length of her throat and the long, sleek lines of her thighs.

Desire flamed through him, an urgent hunger that disgusted him.

He eased her off his lap and onto the bed. Once more she made a soft noise of protest, reaching out for him before her hand fell laxly onto the cover and she seemed to slip into a deeper sleep.

Frowning, he stood and surveyed her. He couldn't leave her like that—it would do her no good for her to sleep in saturated clothes.

So what the *hell* was he to do next?

The next morning, a little shaky but free from fever, Hani blessed modern medications and wondered who her rescuer—so very judgemental—had been. Kelt Gillan...

An unusual name for an unusual man. She could vaguely remember him picking her up, but after that was a blank, though with an odd little shiver she thought she'd never forget his voice, so cold and unsympathetic as he'd—what?

Ordered her to do something. Oh yes, of course. *Swallow the pills.* She gave a weak smile and lifted herself up on her elbow to check the time.

And realised she was in one of the loose cotton shifts she wore at night.

'How—?' she said aloud, a frown pleating her forehead. She sat up, and stared around the room. The dress she'd worn to the party was draped over the chair beside the wardrobe.

Colour burned her skin and she pressed her hands over her eyes. Her rescuer—whoever he was—must have not only stayed with her until the fever broke, but also changed her wet clothes.

Well, she was grateful, she decided sturdily. He'd done what was necessary, and although she cringed at the thought of him seeing and handling her almost naked body, it was obscurely comforting that he'd cared for her.

But for the rest of that day his angular, handsome face was never far from her mind, and with it came a reckless, potent thrill. Trying to reason it into submission didn't work. Instead of her wondering why she reacted so powerfully to the stranger when any other man's closeness repulsed her, the thought of his touch summoned treacherously tantalising thoughts.

Dim recollections of strong arms and a warmth that almost kept at bay the icy grip of the fever made her flush, a heat that faded when into her head popped another vagrant memory— the contempt in his tone when he'd asked her if she was drunk or drugged.

Although she'd never see him again, so she didn't care a bit what he thought of her…

## CHAPTER TWO

THREE weeks later and several thousand kilometres further south, standing on a deck that overlooked a sweep of sand and a cooler Pacific Ocean than she was accustomed to, Hani scanned the faces of the five children in front of her. Though they ranged from a dark-haired, dark-eyed, copper-skinned beauty of about fourteen to a blond little boy slathered with so much sunscreen that his white skin glistened, their features showed they were closely related.

What would it be like to have a family—children of her own?

Her heart twisted and she repressed the thought. Not going to happen, ever.

It was the small blond boy who asked, 'What's your name?'

'Hannah,' she said automatically.

Her accent must have confused them, because the older girl said, 'Honey? That's a nice name.'

And the little boy nodded. 'Your skin's the same colour as honey. Is that why your mum called you that?'

In Tukuulu she'd been Hannah; she liked Honey better. Stifling the hard-won caution that told her it might also confuse anyone too curious, she said cheerfully, 'Actually, it's Hannah, but you can call me Honey if you want to. Now I've told you my name, you'd better tell me yours.'

They all blurted them out together, of course, but six years of teaching infants had instilled a few skills and she soon sorted them out. Hani asked the older girl, 'Kura, where do you live?'

'At Kiwinui,' she said importantly, clearly expecting everyone to know where Kiwinui was. When she realised it meant nothing to Hani, she added, 'It's in the next bay, but we're allowed to walk over the hill and come down here to play if we ask nicely. So we're asking.'

It would take a harder heart than Hani's to withstand the impact of five pairs of expectant eyes. 'I need to know first how good you are at swimming.'

'We're not going to swim because we have to have a grown-up with us when we do that,' Kura told her. 'Mum said so, and The Duke told us off when he caught us only paddling here, and the water only came up to our ankles.'

The *Duke*? Her tone invested the nickname with capitals and indicated that nobody messed with the man, whoever he was.

Curious, Hani asked, 'Who is the duke?'

They looked almost shocked. Kura explained, 'That's like being a prince or something. His nan wears a crown and when she dies his brother will be a duke too and he'll live in a big stone castle on a hill.' She turned and pointed to the headland behind them. 'He lives up there behind the pohutu-kawa trees.'

The Duke's brother, or The Duke? Hani repressed a smile. 'I'm happy for you to play here. Just come and tell me when you're going home again.'

With a whoop they set off, except for the small blond boy, whose name was Jamie. 'Why have you got green eyes?' he asked, staring at her.

'Because my mother had green eyes.' Hani repressed a familiar pang of pain. She and her brother had both inherited those eyes; every time she looked in the mirror she thought of Rafiq.

Surely she should be reconciled to never seeing him again by now!

Jamie nodded. 'They're nice. Why are you staying here?'

'I'm on holiday.' The day after her last attack of fever the principal had told her that if she didn't take up the offer to go to New Zealand—'long enough to get this fever out of your system'—the charity that ran the school couldn't accept responsibility for her welfare. Her air fares would be paid, and the beach house where she'd convalesce was rent-free.

Without exactly stating that they'd terminate her employment if she didn't go, he'd implied it so strongly she'd been persuaded to reluctantly leave the safety of Tukuulu.

Curiosity satisfied, Jamie said nonchalantly, 'See you later,' and scampered off to join the others.

Hani sat back down in the comfortable wicker chair on the deck. Airy and casually luxurious, the beach house was surprisingly big, with glass doors in every room opening out onto a wide wooden deck that overlooked the cove. Her landlord, an elderly man, had met her flight the previous night and driven her here to what he'd called a bach.

Remembering his very English accent, she smiled. No doubt those cut-glass vowels were why the children had decided he must be some sort of aristocrat.

After introducing himself very formally as Arthur Wellington, he'd said, 'The refrigerator and the pantry have been stocked with staples. If you need anything else, do ring the number on the calendar beside the telephone.'

Hani thanked him for that, but realised now that she'd missed telling him how much she appreciated being given the opportunity to stay here.

She'd do that when she paid him for the groceries he'd supplied.

On a long, soft sigh she took her gaze away from the children long enough to examine the cove. Sand like amber suede curved against the kingfisher expanse of water. Squinting against the bright sky, Hani eyed the headland where the landlord lived. Its steep slopes were hidden by more of the dark-leafed trees that lined the beach, their massive limbs swooping down over the sand.

A formal house to match her landlord's formal manner? She hoped not. It would look incongruous in this pristinely beautiful scene.

Loud shrieks from the beach dragged her attention back to the game taking place in front of the bach, one that involved much yelling, more laughter, and some frenzied racing around. For the first time in months she felt a stirring of energy.

Smiling, checking that little Jamie didn't get too close to the water, she failed to notice an intruder until he was almost at the cottage. The soft clink of harness alerting her, she swivelled around and saw a horse—a fine bay, strong enough to take its tall, powerfully built rider without effort.

Her startled gaze took in the rider. He sat easily on his mount—but that wasn't why her pulses revved into overdrive.

For a second—just long enough to terrify and delight her— he reminded her of her brother. Rafiq had the same coiled grace of strength and litheness, the same relaxed control of his mount.

The same air of authority.

Then she recalled when she'd seen this man before, and an odd, baseless panic froze the breath in her throat. In spite of the bout of fever she'd been suffering when she met him on Tukuulu, those hard-hewn features and hooded eyes were sharply etched into her memory.

As was the feel of his arms around her... And the knowledge that he'd stripped her saturated clothes from her and somehow managed to get her into the loose shift she wore at night.

What the *hell* was he doing here?

He swung down, looped the reins over a fencepost and opened the gate to come towards her. Subliminally intimidated by the arrogant angle of his head and the smooth, lethal grace of his stride, Hani forced herself to her feet, stiffening her spine and her knees.

Although tall for a woman, she couldn't match him. Her chin came up; unsmiling, breath locking in her throat, she watched him approach while a feverish awareness lifted the invisible hairs on the back of her neck.

He was—well, *gorgeous* was the only word she could come up with. Except that gorgeous made her think of male models, and this man looked like no male model she'd ever seen. That effortless, inborn air of command hardened his already bold features into an intimidating mask of force and power, emphasised by a cold steel-blue gaze and a thinning of his subtly sensuous mouth.

He was handsome enough to make any woman's heart shake—even one as frozen as hers—but something uncompromising and formidable about him set off alarms in every nerve.

He had to be The Duke. A swift stab of apprehension screwed her nerves even tighter. Felipe, the man she'd once thought she loved, had called himself a French count.

It was stupid of her, but the children's innocent misconception seemed somehow ominous.

Hani knew she should be relieved when he looked at her with a total lack of male interest. Scarily, she wasn't.

OK, so the last thing she wanted was a man to see her as

a sexual being, but... On Tukuulu he'd noticed her as a woman; now he looked at her with complete indifference.

And that stung.

Trying to keep this meeting on a sensible basis, she said warily, 'Hello. I didn't realise that you owned this place. Thank you so much for letting me stay here.'

'I hoped to see you looking a bit better,' he said curtly.

'I am much better.' Yes, her voice was fine—crisp, just as cool and impersonal as his, a far cry from her slurred tone that night at the ceremony. Meeting his merciless survey with an assumption of confidence, she hid her uncertainty with a shrug. 'Another thing I have to thank you for is your rescue of me.'

One black brow lifted. 'It was nothing; I happened to be the closest person around.'

Heat tinged her skin. Trying to sound professional and assured, she said crisply, 'It was very kind of you. I don't remember much—' only the sound of his voice, calm and re-assuring, and the wonderful comfort of his arms when he'd held her until the shivering stopped '—but I know I didn't change myself.'

His eyes narrowed slightly. 'Once the fever had broken I went back to the school dance floor, but everyone had gone by then. It didn't seem a good idea for you to sleep in wet clothes, so I removed your dress.' In a coldly formidable tone, he finished, 'I behaved as a brother might have.'

Colour burned into her skin. Hoping her words mingled the right blend of gratitude and distance, she said, 'Yes—well, I thought as much.' And then, changing the subject without finesse, 'Thanks again for being generous ºnough to let me stay in this lovely place.'

'You've thanked me enough,' he said a little curtly, adding with a faint smile, 'I went to school with your principal. When he asked if his teachers could use this bach I agreed. It's not used very often, and it seems a waste to have it sit here empty. You're the third teacher to come here, and I expect there will be others.'

So that was the connection. And he was making sure she didn't think she was special.

She said with cool assurance, 'I'm grateful. But to make things very clear, I was neither drunk nor drugged that night in Tukuulu.'

One straight black brow lifted. 'I wondered if you'd remember that. I'm sorry for jumping to conclusions—it didn't take me long to realise you were ill.'

For some reason she wasn't prepared to explore, she didn't want his apology. 'I sent you a letter thanking you for your help.'

'Yes, your principal passed it on.'

He hadn't answered. Well, for heaven's sake, she hadn't expected him to.

Without inflection, he said, 'I'm glad I was there when you needed someone. I'm Kelt Crysander-Gillan—although I don't use the first part of my surname—and I live just up the hill.'

Nothing about being some sort of aristocrat, she noted. Clearly The Duke was just a nickname, perhaps because of the double-barrelled name. They mightn't be common in New Zealand.

And he *looked* like a duke, someone of importance, his very presence a statement of authority. A very sexy duke, sexier than any other duke she'd ever met...

One who'd taken her clothes off and seen her naked...

Firmly she tamped down a sizzle of adrenalin. 'And of course you know that I'm Han-*Hannah* Court.'

Oh, he'd really unnerved her! For the first time in years

she'd almost given him her real name, catching it back only just in time. Startled, she automatically held out her hand.

'Welcome to New Zealand,' he said gravely, and his long, lean fingers closed around hers.

Her heart picked up speed. *Cool it*, she commanded her runaway pulse fiercely while he shook hands.

There was no reason for the swift sizzle of sensation that shocked her every nerve. Acting on pure blind instinct, Hani jerked her hand free.

Kelt Gillan's brows met for a taut second above his blade of a nose, but he turned when the children chose that moment to surge up from the beach, their shouted greetings a melee of sound.

He silenced them with a crisp, 'All right, calm down, you lot.'

She expected them to shuffle their feet, but although they obediently stayed silent their wide smiles told her he was popular with them.

Amazing, she thought, watching as he said something to each of them. And again she remembered Felipe, her first and only lover. He'd had no time for children; there was no profit to be made from them…

Kelt Gillan said, 'Miss Court has been ill and needs a lot of rest, so I want you to play on the homestead beach until she's better.'

Their attention swivelled back to her.

Into the silence Jamie said earnestly, 'I was sick too, Honey. I had mumps and my throat was sore and I couldn't eat anything 'cept ice cream and jelly and scrambled eggs.'

'And soup,' the lovely Kura reminded him officiously.

He pulled a face. 'And some soup.'

'I'm getting much better now,' Hani said, smiling at him. 'And I'm lucky—I can eat anything I like.'

'Honey?' Kelt said on an upward inflection, that taunting brow lifting again as his cool gaze inspected her face. 'I thought your name was Hannah?'

'I'll have to learn to talk like a New Zealander,' she said lightly, irritated by the colour that heated her cheekbones. In the last six years she'd worked hard to banish any vestige of the soft cadences of her birth country.

'Actually, it suits you,' he said, a sardonic note colouring his deep voice. He turned back to the children. 'All right, off you go.'

They turned obediently, all but Jamie. 'Where do you live?' he asked Hani.

Nowhere… 'On a hot little island called Tukuulu a long way over the sea from here.'

An older girl, Jamie's, sister—cousin?—turned. 'Come *on*, Jamie,' she commanded importantly, and the boy gave Hani a swift grin and scampered off.

'What charming children. Are they siblings?' she asked into the suddenly oppressive silence.

'Siblings and cousins. In New Zealand the term *whanau* is used to denote the extended family,' the man beside her said.

'You didn't need to warn them off,' she told him. 'I like children.'

Kelt Gillan said succinctly, 'Honey or Hannah or whoever you are, you're here to convalesce, and it's no part of that healing process to act as unpaid babysitter. Your principal asked me to make sure you didn't overexert yourself.'

His words set off a flicker of memory. The night he'd unhooked her from the coconut palm and carried her home he'd spoken in exactly that controlled, uncompromising tone. As though she were an idiot, she thought angrily.

She didn't care what Kelt thought, but it wasn't fair to

spoil the children's pleasure. 'Both you and he are very thoughtful, but I'm quite capable of making decisions like that for myself. Believe me, it didn't hurt me or tire me or worry me to sit in the sun and watch them. I enjoyed it.'

'Perhaps so,' he said inflexibly, 'but that's not the point. You're here to rest and regain your strength. I'll make sure their parents understand that they stay in Homestead Bay. Don't fret about curtailing their fun—they'll play quite happily there.'

Behind him his horse lifted its head from lipping the grass and took a step sideways, its powerful muscles fluid beneath satiny skin.

In Moraze, her homeland, herds of wild horses roamed the grassy plateau country that surrounded the central volcanic peaks. Descended from Arabian steeds, they'd been brought there by her ancestor, a renegade French aristocrat who'd settled the island with a rag-tag train of soldiers and a beautiful Arabian wife.

Hani's parents had given her one of those horses for her third birthday…

Long dead, her parents and that first gentle mount, and it was years since she'd ridden.

Hani was ambushed by a pang of homesickness, an aching sense of loss so fierce it must have shown in her face.

'Sit down!' Kelt said sharply, unable to stop himself from taking a step towards her.

One hand came up, warning him off. Apart from that abrupt gesture she didn't move, and the flash of something tight and almost desperate in her expression disappeared. Her black hair swirled around her shoulders in a cloud of fiery highlights as she angled her chin at him.

Looking him straight in the eye, she said in a gentle voice with a distinct edge to it, 'Mr Gillan, I'm neither an invalid nor a child. I make my own decisions and I'm perfectly capable of looking after myself.'

He examined her closely, but her lovely face was shut against him, that moment of despair—if that was what it had been—replaced by aloof self-assurance.

Kelt chose to live in New Zealand for his own good reasons, one of them being that Kiwinui had been in his grandfather's family for over a hundred years, and he felt a deep emotional link to the place. But as a scion of the royal family of Carathia he'd been born to command. Backed by their grandmother, the Grand Duchess, he and his brother had turned their backs on tradition and gone into business together as soon as he'd left university. Between them they'd built up a hugely successful enterprise, a leader in its field that had made them both billionaires.

Women had chased him mercilessly since he'd left school. Although none had touched his heart, he treated his mistresses with courtesy, and had somehow acquired a legendary status as a lover.

Women were an open book to him.

Until now. One part of him wanted to tell Hannah Court that while she was on Kiwinui she was under his protection; the other wanted to sweep that elegant body into his arms and kiss her perfect mouth into submission.

Instead, he said crisply, 'And I'll do what I consider to be best for the situation. If you need anything, there's a contact number by the telephone.'

Hani looked at him with cool, unreadable green eyes, the colour of New Zealand's most precious greenstone. 'Thank you; Mr Wellington told me about that.'

Kelt shrugged. 'Arthur works for me.'

Her head inclined almost regally. 'I see.'

'Tell me if another bout of fever hits you.'

'It's not necessary—I have medication to deal with it.' Another hint of soft apricot tinged her exotic cheekbones when she continued, 'As you found out, it works very quickly.'

Clearly, she had no intention of giving an inch. He wondered how old she was—mid-twenties, he guessed, but something in her bearing and the direct glance of those amazing eyes reminded him of his grandmother, the autocratic Grand Duchess who'd kept her small realm safe through wars and threats for over fifty years.

Dismissing such a ridiculous thought, he said, 'Do you drive?'

'Of course.' Again that hint of appraisal in her tone, in her gaze.

'Any idea of New Zealand's road rules?' he asked, making no attempt to hide the ironic note in his voice.

'I'm a quick learner. But how far is it to the nearest village? If it's close enough I can walk there when I need anything.'

'It's about five kilometres—too far for you to walk in the summer heat.'

Warily wondering if he'd given up any idea of looking after her—because he seemed like a man with an over-developed protective streak and a strong will—she pointed out, 'I'm used to heat.'

'If that were true, you wouldn't be convalescing here.' And while she was absorbing that dig, he went on, 'And somehow I doubt very much that you're accustomed to walking five kilometres while carrying groceries.'

Uneasily aware of the unsettling glint in his cold blue eyes, Hani shrugged. 'Don't worry about me, Mr Gillan. I won't be a bother to anyone.'

A single black brow climbed, but all he said was, 'Call me Kelt. Most New Zealanders are very informal.'

She most emphatically didn't want to call him anything! However, she'd already established her independence, so, hiding her reluctance, she returned courteously, 'Then you must call me Hannah.'

He lifted one black brow. 'You know, I think I prefer Honey. Hannah is—very Victorian. And you're not.'

The slight—very slight—pause before he said Victorian made her wonder if he'd been going to say virginal.

If so, he couldn't be more wrong.

Far from virginal, far from Victorian, she thought with an aching regret. 'I'd prefer Hannah, thank you.'

His smile was tinged by irony. 'Hannah it shall be. If you feel up to it, I'd like you to come to dinner tomorrow night.'

Caution warned her to prevaricate, fudge the truth a little and say she wasn't well enough to socialise, but she'd already cut off that avenue of escape when she'd made it clear she didn't need to be looked after by—well, by *anyone*, she thought sturdily.

Especially not this man, whose unyielding maleness affected her so strongly she could feel his impact on every cell. Even politely setting limits as she'd just done had energised her, set her senses tingling, and every time she looked into that hard, handsome face she felt a hot, swift tug of—of lust, she reminded herself bitterly.

And she knew—only too well—what that could lead to.

However, he was her landlord. She owed him for several things; his impersonal care on Tukuulu, the refrigerator full of groceries.

Changing her wet clothes…

Ignoring the deep-seated pulse of awareness, she said, 'That's very kind of you. What time would you like me to be there?'

'I'll pick you up at seven,' he told her with another keen glance. 'Until then, take things slowly.'

His long-legged strides across the lawn presented her with a disturbing view of broad shoulders and narrow hips above lean, heavily muscled thighs. He dressed well too—his trousers had been tailored for him, and she'd almost bet his shirt had too.

Very sexy, she thought frivolously, quelling the liquid heat that consumed her. Some lucky men were born with that *it* factor, a compelling masculinity that attracted every female eye.

And she'd bet the subject of her letting someone know if she had another attack of fever would come up again.

A few paces away he swivelled, catching her intent, fascinated look. A challenge flared in his narrowed eyes; he understood exactly what effect he was having on her.

Hot with shame, she wanted to turn away, but Kelt held her gaze for a second, his own enigmatic and opaque.

However, when he spoke his voice was crisp and aloof. 'If you need anything, let me know.'

It sounded like a classical *double entendre*; if he'd been Felipe it would have been.

It was time she stopped judging men by Felipe's standards. The years in Tukuulu had shown her that most men were not like him, and there was no reason to believe that Kelt Gillan wasn't a perfectly decent farmer with a face like one of the more arrogant gods, an overdeveloped protective instinct and more than his share of formidable male presence.

'Thank you—I will,' she said remotely.

And produced a smile she held until he'd swung up onto his horse and guided it away.

Her face felt frozen when she took refuge in the cottage and stood listening as the sound of hooves dwindled into the warm, sea-scented air. She shivered, crossing her arms and rubbing her hands over her prickling skin.

*Again?* she thought in mindless panic. The unbidden, unwanted surge of sensual appetite humiliated her. Why on earth was she attracted to dangerous men?

Not that she'd realised Felipe was dangerous when she first met him. And for some unfounded and quite illogical reason she couldn't believe Kelt would turn out to be like Felipe.

As well, the heady clamour Kelt Gillan summoned in her was different—more earthy and primal, nothing like the fascinated excitement she'd felt when Felipe had pursued her. He'd seemed such a glamorous, fascinating man, with his French title and his famous friends. At eighteen she'd been so green she'd run headlong into peril without a second thought.

Six years older, and much better able to look after herself, she sensed a different danger in Kelt Gillan—a more elemental attraction without the calculation that had marked Felipe's seduction.

Desperate to take her mind off her enigmatic landlord and his unnerving effect on her, she went across to the kitchen and put on the electric kettle.

'Displacement activity,' she said aloud, a mirthless smile curling her mouth as she spooned coffee into the plunger.

Wrapping her attraction to Felipe in a romantic haze had got her into deep trouble; this time she'd face her inconvenient response to Kelt Gillan squarely. Coffee mug in hand, she walked out onto the deck and stood looking out over the sea.

No emotions, no fooling herself that this was love, no silly claptrap about soulmates. She'd already been down that track and it had led to humiliation and heartbreak and terror. Felipe had played on her naivety, setting himself out to charm her into submission.

And succeeding utterly, so that she'd gradually been manipulated into an affair without fully realising where she was
heading. When she'd realised what sort of man he was she'd
tried to break away, only to have him bind her to him with the
cruellest, most degrading chains. To free herself she'd had to
sacrifice everything—self-respect, love for her brother, her
very future.

Closing her eyes against the dazzling shimmer of the sun
on the bay, she thought wearily that she hadn't planned for
her sacrifice to last the rest of her life.

In fact, she hadn't planned on any further life.

Well, a Mediterranean fisherman with smuggling as a
sideline had seen to it that she'd survived. She shivered, and
for a foolish few seconds wondered if Kelt Gillan had brought
on another attack of fever.

No, her chill was due to memories she wished she could
banish.

Only right now she needed them to remind her that no
person could ever see into the heart of another, especially
when they were blinded by lust.

Ruthlessly she dragged her mind back to the present, and concentrated on the problem at hand—her feelings for Kelt Gillan.

'Just think rationally,' she told herself.

What she felt when she looked at Kelt was a powerful
physical attraction for a man both formidable and enormously attractive—a primal arousal with a scientific basis.
Humans instinctively recognised the people they'd make
superb babies with.

Logic played no part in it, nor did common sense. But
both could be used as weapons against it, and if she'd learned
anything these past six years it was that any relationship
between lovers needed much more than desire to be a success.

And there would be no babies for her, ever.

So she'd have dinner with Kelt and then she'd stay well away from him.

Hani missed the children the next day, and not for the first time wondered what on earth she was going to do for three months. Too many empty weeks stretched before her, leaving her far too much time to think, to remember. Without the steady routine of school she faced more than simple boredom; she'd have to deal with emptiness.

At least the cottage had a set of bookshelves stuffed with books of all ages and quite a few magazines. After a brief walk along the beach that reminded her again how unfit she was, she sank into a chair on the deck with a cup of tea and a volume on New Zealand that looked interesting.

She flicked it open and saw a bookplate. Kelt Crysander-Gillan, it stated.

'Unusual,' she said aloud. There was an inscription too, but she turned the page on that, feeling as though she was prying.

With a name like that, and if Kelt's air of forceful authority had led to a nickname like The Duke, imaginative children could well come up with a crown-wearing grandmother somewhere in Europe.

At precisely seven o'clock he arrived to collect her as the sun was dipping behind the forest-covered mountains that ran down the central spine of Northland's long, narrow peninsula. He drove a large, luxurious four-wheel-drive, which gave Hani a moment of heart-sickness; her brother used to drive the same make...

Hani pushed the thought to the back of her mind. Rafiq thought she was dead, and that was the way she had to stay.

And then Kelt got out, lithe and long-legged, powerfully

magnetic and urbane in a short-sleeved shirt that echoed the steely colour of his eyes, and casually elegant trousers, and the bitter, heart-sick memories vanished, replaced by a reckless excitement.

When he opened the gate she went hastily out into the serene evening. The bach might be his, but she didn't want to sense his dominating presence whenever she walked into the living room.

She knew she looked good. For an hour that afternoon she'd pored over her scanty wardrobe, startled to find herself wistfully remembering her favourites amongst the designer clothes she'd worn in her old life.

In the end she'd chosen a modest dress she'd found in a shop in Tukuulu's small capital city. Although it was a little too loose on her, the clear salmon hue burnished the gold of her skin and the warm highlights in her dark hair.

Tempted to go without make-up, she decided after a critical survey of her reflection that a naked face might make her look conspicuous, and her security depended on blending in. So she compromised on lipstick a slightly deeper shade than her dress, and pinned her badly cut hair off her face with two frangipani clips made from the moonbeam shimmer of pearl shell.

Kelt waited for her beside the gate. Her shoulders held a little stiffly to hide an absurd self-consciousness, she walked towards him, sensing a darker, more elemental level beneath his coolly sophisticated exterior. Trying to ignore the smouldering need in the pit of her stomach, she saw him as a warrior, riding his big bay gelding into battle...

Not, she thought with an inner shiver, a man to cross swords with.

With a carefully neutral smile she met his gaze, and in a

charged moment her wilful memory sabotaged the fragile
veneer of her composure by supplying a repeat of how it had
felt when he'd carried her—the powerful litheness of his gait,
the subtle flexion of his body as he'd lifted her, his controlled
strength…

# CHAPTER THREE

KELT examined her face with the impersonal keenness of a doctor. 'How are you?' he asked, opening the door of the car.

Hani's smile faded. His persistent view of her as an invalid was—*demeaning*, she decided on a spurt of irritation that didn't quite mask a deeper, more dangerous emotion. After all, in the light of her unexpected attraction, it was far safer if he saw her as an invalid than as a woman.

A desirable woman.

With a hint of frost in her tone she answered, 'Fine, thank you.' And met his scrutiny with head held high and an immobile face that belied the unsteady rhythm of her heart.

'You still have dark circles under your eyes. Lack of sleep?'

Strangely enough, for the first time since she'd come to this side of the world all those years ago she'd slept deeply and dreamlessly, waking with an energy that seemed alien.

'No, not at all,' she told him evenly. Steering the conversation away from her illness, she asked, 'How far away is your house?'

'About a kilometre by road; half that distance if you walk across the paddocks—which I don't want you to do.' He set the car in motion.

'Why?'

He sent her a narrow glance. 'You could spook the cattle.' After a pause, he added, 'Or they might spook you.'

Hani examined some large, square animals, their coats glowing deep red-gold in the rays of the evening sun. 'They don't *look* excitable, but your point is well taken.'

Not that she planned to be going cross-country.

'And you?' he asked levelly, turning across a cattle grid.

She waited until the rattling died away before saying, 'I don't understand.'

'Are you excitable?'

Startled, she looked across at him, saw an enigmatic smile tuck in the corners of his hard mouth, and was shocked again by a fierce tug of arousal, sweet as honey, dangerous as dynamite.

Surely he wasn't *flirting* with her?

She felt winded and fascinated at the same time until a moment's reflection produced sanity. Of course he wasn't coming on to her. Not unless he was the sort of man who indulged in meaningless flirtations with any available woman.

Somehow she didn't want to believe he'd be so indiscriminate. A man with Kelt Gillan's effortless masculinity could have any woman he wanted, and he must know it. And unlike Felipe he had nothing to gain from seducing her.

In her most sedate tone she said, 'Not in the least. Teachers can't afford to be volatile. It's *very* bad for discipline.'

That should tell him she wasn't in the market for a holiday affair. To clinch it, she said, 'Don't worry, I won't walk in your fields or excite your cattle.'

'Paddocks,' he said laconically, explaining, 'New Zealanders call anything with animals in it a paddock. *Fields* are what we play sport on, and as far as we're concerned meadows don't exist.' He nodded at the setting sun. 'And that range of hills to the west is covered in native bush, not forest or woods.'

Intrigued, she said, 'I do know about bush. One of the Australian teachers at the school explained it to me. It's fascinating how countries colonised by the same power could develop such different words to describe things. In South Africa—'

She stopped suddenly, her mind freezing in dismay, then hastily tried to cover the slip by asking the first question that came to mind. 'What are those trees, the ones that grow in groups in nearly all your f—paddocks?'

'They're totara trees.'

'Oh. Do they flower?'

'Not noticeably—they're conifers. As for terminology— well, the world would be a boring place if we were all the same. Settlers in different countries adjusted to different conditions.' He paused a beat before adding casually, 'You're not South African, are you?'

'No,' she said, dry-throated.

'But clearly you've been there.'

Trying to banish any reluctance from her voice, she admitted, 'I spent a holiday there when I was young.'

He accepted that without comment. 'So what made a young Englishwoman decide to spend years teaching in a village school in a place like Tukuulu? The lure of tropical islands I can understand, but once you'd got to Tukuulu and realised it's really nothing but a volcano with a huge mine on it— beaches of dead coral, only one fleapit of a hotel, no night life—what kept you there?'

A little shudder tightened her skin, but she kept her gaze fixed steadily ahead. Let him probe as much as he liked; she had her story down pat.

'I wanted to help. And they were desperate for teachers. It's really hard for them to keep staff. But the principal is your friend so you must know that.'

After a moment's pause he said, 'How long do you plan to live there?'

'For several years yet,' she evaded.

'I imagine it's unusual for anyone to stay for long in a Pacific backwater like Tukuulu.' Let alone a young Englishwoman, his tone implied.

'You're a sophisticated man but you don't seem to mind living on a remote cattle station in a Pacific backwater like New Zealand,' she retorted sweetly.

He gave her swift, ironic smile. 'Don't let any New Zealander hear you call the place a backwater. We're a proud people with plenty to be proud of.'

'The Tukuuluans are proud too, and doing their best to move into the modern world without losing the special things that make their culture so distinctive.'

'I suspect that's an impossible task,' he said cynically.

'I hope not. And I like to think I'm helping them in a small way.'

They crossed another cattle grid and drove through a grove of the big trees she'd noticed before, their great branches almost touching the ground.

'Oh,' she exclaimed in involuntary pleasure, 'the leaves are silver underneath! From a distance the trees look so sombre— yet how pretty they must be when there's any wind.'

'Very, and when they flower in a month or so they'll be great torches of scarlet and crimson and maroon. I'll take you over the top of the hill so you can look over Kiwinui and get some idea of the lie of the land.'

Kelt slowed the vehicle to a stop, switching off the engine so that the silence flowed in around them, bringing with it the sweet scent of damp grass and the ever-present salt of the sea.

Gaze fixed in front of her, Hani said on an indrawn breath, 'This is glorious.'

'Yes.'

That was all, but his controlled voice couldn't hide the pride of ownership as he gazed out at his vast domain.

At the foot of the hill a sweeping bay fronted a large, almost flat, grassed area with what appeared to be a small settlement to one side. More huge trees fringed the beach and a long jetty stitched its way out into the water towards a sleek black yacht and a large motorboat.

'The working part of Kiwinui,' Kelt told her. He leaned slightly towards her so he could point. 'Cattle yards, the woolshed, implement sheds and the workers' cottages.'

Hani's breath stopped in her throat. He was too close, so near she could see the fine grain of his tanned skin, so close her nostrils were teased by a faint, wholly male scent. Hot little shivers snaked down her spine, and some locked, previously untouched part of her splintered into shards.

Desperate to overcome the clamour of her response, she scrambled from the car and took a couple of steps away. When Kelt joined her she didn't dare look at him.

Several measured breaths helped calm her racing heartbeats, and as soon as she could trust her voice she waved a hand at the nearest hill. 'What's that mown strip over there?'

'An airstrip. Kiwinui is too big to fertilise except from the air.' His words held a lick of amusement, as though he had sensed her stormy reaction to him and found it entertaining.

Mortified and bewildered, Hani wondered if the forced intimacy of their first meeting had somehow forged this—this wild physical reaction.

Yes, that had to be it. Relief eased her shame; her response was not some weird aberration or a frightening return to the servitude of her affair with Felipe. Kelt had held her closely, given her comfort while she fought the fever—changed her clothes—so naturally her body and mind responded to his presence.

Well, they could stop it right now. Discipline was what was needed here. She didn't want to feel like this every time she saw him, completely unable to control herself!

Trying to block out his presence, she concentrated on the view. To the north a series of ranges scalloped the coast, the lower-slopes pasture, the gullies and heights covered by forests—no, *native bush*—that reminded her of the jungles of Moraze. Between them she glimpsed a coast of sandy beaches and more green paddocks.

Stretching to the eastern horizon was the restless sea, its kingfisher-coloured expanse broken by a large, high island that formed an offshore barrier.

And, to cap it all, she heard the high, exquisite trill of a bird, joy rendered into song that soared into the golden light of the setting sun. Pierced by sudden delight, Hani dragged in a long breath.

And even as she thrilled to it, she knew that the man beside her somehow intensified her mood, her appreciation, as though his presence had the power to magnify her responses.

Felipe had never done that.

Hani swallowed. 'It's so beautiful,' she managed. 'What's the bird that's singing?'

He gave her a sharp look. 'It's a thrush,' he said. 'They were introduced here by the early settlers. He'll be perched on top of one of the pohutukawa trees.'

*Bother*, she thought on a surge of irrational panic, oh, bother and double-bother! Too late she remembered a poem she'd learned at school; if she were as English as her accent she'd probably recognise a thrush's song...

On the other hand, why should Kelt be suspicious? And even if he was, he wouldn't be able to find out who she was. Once she'd escaped Felipe she'd covered her tracks so well that even he, with all his resources in brutal men and tainted money, hadn't been able to hunt her down.

Kelt told her, 'The original homestead was down on the flat, quite close to the workers' cottages you can see, but when it burned down early in the twentieth century the new one was built up here.'

Hani filed away the fact that in New Zealand—at least in the countryside—substantial houses were called cottages. 'What's the difference between a cottage and a homestead and a bach?'

'A bach is a holiday cottage, always casual, very beachy. They used to be small and primitive, but nowadays that isn't necessarily so.'

'No indeed,' she said, thinking of the bach she was staying in.

He gave her an ironic smile. 'My grandmother made quite a few renovations to it. She enjoyed the simple life for a short time, but had no intention of giving up any comfort.'

His grandmother had clearly been a sophisticate. Well, Kiwinui was a big farm, and Hani didn't need to know the size of his bank balance to accept that Kelt was a wealthy man.

Kelt said, 'As for workers' cottages, the term's a hangover from the days when they were fairly basic. Nowadays no worker would be happy with basic housing, and even if he was his wife certainly wouldn't be, so they're usually good-sized family homes.'

'And a homestead is where the owner of the farm lives?' she guessed.

'Either the owner or manager's house on a farm or station.'

Hani nodded. 'Is this estate—Kiwinui—a farm or a station? What's the difference?'

'Basically a station is a larger farm—usually settled early in New Zealand's history. The first Gillan arrived here about a hundred and forty years ago. And yes, Kiwinui is a station.'

Hani looked down at the bay, frowning at the abrupt change of colour in the water. 'It looks as though it gets deep very quickly there,' she observed. 'Surely my cove—' colouring, she hastily corrected herself '—I mean, the one with the bach, would be safer for the children? I truly don't mind them coming, and I'd be happy to supervise their swimming. And young Kura seems very capable.'

'We'll see how things go.' His tone was non-committal. 'When those dark circles disappear then perhaps the children can pay you visits.'

Hani sent him a sharp look. 'The darkness under my eyes will go in its own good time. And I enjoy children's company.'

'You'll enjoy it more when you're stronger.'

His tone left no room for negotiation. Fuming, Hani decided that autocratic wasn't emphatic enough to describe him. Clearly he was accustomed to giving orders and seeing them obeyed.

And yet—she didn't feel suffocated as she had when she'd fancied herself in love with Felipe.

But then, after the first few times she'd never argued with Felipe. Unpleasant things happened to those who crossed him.

Chilled, she turned to get back into the car.

Kelt retraced their path, turning off over a cattle grid when they reached the drive to the homestead. More great trees shaded them, deciduous ones with fresh green foliage. Amongst them she recognised a flame tree, and a pang of homesickness tore through her, so painful she bit her lip and turned her head away. On Moraze the flame trees bloomed like a cloak of fire across the island…

You'll never see Moraze again, she reminded herself starkly.

Kelt's fingers tightened on the wheel. The sheen of moisture in her great green eyes struck at something fundamental in him. Just what the hell was going on inside that black head with its gleaming fiery highlights?

Probably nothing more than a lack of control due to her prolonged illness.

Yet behind Hannah Court's cool, serene facade he sensed something stronger, more deeply emotional than a physical weakness, and had to repress an urgent desire to tell her that whatever her problems, he'd probably be able to help.

This fierce urge to protect was something new, and he distrusted it. Because he avoided breaking hearts, he'd always made sure his lovers had been capable of looking after themselves.

Damn it, he didn't want to lust after a woman who was here to recuperate from a severe bout of tropical fever. So it was infuriating that he couldn't prise the image of Hannah, sleek and desirable in the hot, tropical night, from his mind. He felt like some lecherous voyeur.

Abruptly he asked, 'How long have you been driving?'

Her brows lifted, but she answered mildly enough. 'Since I was sixteen.'

For some reason—one he wasn't prepared to examine— her dismissive tone exasperated Kelt. 'And do you have an international licence?'

'Yes.'

He braked as they came up to the portico of his home. 'I'll lend you a vehicle, but you'd better read New Zealand's road rules before you take it out.'

She gave him a startled glance. 'That's very kind of you, but—'

'That way you'll be independent,' he said coolly.

Hani chided herself for feeling deflated. Naturally he wouldn't want a total stranger relying on him for transport. Yet her pride baulked at accepting the use of a car.

'Are you sure? I mean—you don't know anything about me. And lending me a car isn't necessary—'

'I've lent the same car to every other teacher who's stayed at the bach, and so far it hasn't had a scratch.' His tone was amused yet definite. 'If I thought you'd break the mould I wouldn't be offering.'

'I—well, thank you very much.' It didn't seem enough, but all she could think of was to repeat lamely, 'It's very kind of you.'

The vehicle stopped. The warm light of the westering sun emphasised the classical framework of his face as he turned to her. In a voice that gave nothing away, he said, 'Welcome to my home,' before opening the door and getting out.

Awkwardly she unclipped herself and scrambled free, wondering why she'd been so affected by the unsmiling look that accompanied his conventional words.

Cool it, she commanded herself; stop seeing things that don't exist. As with the offer of a car, he wasn't being *personal*. No doubt he said exactly the same words to everyone who came to his house for the first time. She had to stop foolishly seeking hidden meanings in every steel-blue glance, every alteration of tone in the deep voice.

Farming, she decided with a slight shock while she absorbed the full extent of the house, must have been exceedingly profitable during the first quarter of the twentieth century when this was built. The big wooden building had been designed in an Arts and Crafts style that fitted seamlessly into the ageless, almost primeval land and seascape.

Kelt showed no sign of pride when he escorted her to the

door and opened it. Did he take it for granted—as she, in her self-centred youth, had viewed the *castello*, her family home in Moraze?

Trying not to stare around like a tourist, she said, 'This is very beautiful.'

'Thank you,' he responded gravely.

Feeling foolish and gushing, she asked, 'Have you lived here all your life?'

He didn't look at her. 'No.' After a pause so slight she barely noticed he went on, 'My mother wasn't a New Zealander, and I spent quite a lot of time in her country. However, this is my home.'

Another door opened further down, and a middle-aged man came through—her driver from the airport, carrying a large fish in a flax basket. He stopped abruptly.

Absurdly cheered by a familiar face, Hani smiled at him, and said, 'Hello, Mr Wellington. How nice to see you again.'

'Nice to see you again too, Miss Court,' he responded courteously, adding, 'And my name is Arthur.'

Kelt said, 'Hannah thought you owned Kiwinui.'

The older man looked a little taken aback. 'There's only one master here, Miss Court.' His tone indicated she just might have committed sacrilege. He indicated the basket and said, 'I hope you like fish.'

Trying to ease the tension that knotted her nerves, she told him, 'I love it.'

'Good.' He beamed at her. 'This is snapper, freshly caught with my own fair hands today. But when you come next time I'll make sure we have beef—I know it can be difficult to get good beef in some of the smaller islands in the Pacific Ocean.'

'It is, and I'll enjoy it enormously.' Not that she planned to come again…

He nodded and disappeared through another door, presumably into the kitchen.

Kelt indicated a door further down the hall. 'This way.'

The room he took her into opened out onto a terrace; the sun had almost sunk beneath the ranges and the clouds were edged with gold and vivid raspberry and ruby highlights. Hani looked around her, insensibly relaxing in the gracious room, one wall a bank of French windows that opened out onto a terrace. Wide stone steps led down to a lawn surrounded by shrub and flower borders that blended into taller trees.

'Oh, your garden is magnificent.' She gazed across the expanse of stone flagging and took a deep breath, relishing the fresh, summery scent of new-mown grass. Nothing could have been a greater contrast to the school, set in a landscape scarred by its huge mine.

Kelt must have picked up on her thoughts. 'A little different from Tukuulu.'

'A lot different.' This was just an ordinary social occasion, so behave like a normal person, she told herself.

Her appreciative smile faded a little when she met his hooded gaze, but she kept it pinned to her lips. 'Unfortunately the mine is Tukuulu's only source of income.'

'It doesn't look as though its owners care much about their neighbours,' he said austerely.

'I suppose you can't blame them, but—well, most of the mine-workers' children go to the school. You'd think they'd give it some support. That's the problem with big conglomerates owned by people from overseas who have no personal interest in the people they're employing.'

She'd spoken a little heatedly, and he sent her another keen look. Curiosity drove her to ask, 'Was it the first time you'd been to Tukuulu?'

'Yes. Your principal's been suggesting a visit to me for years but it's never been convenient before.'

Hani found it hard to imagine what Kelt had in common with the slightly older man who'd devoted his life to the school he ran on a shoestring.

He went on, 'He needs help, of course, and he'll probably get it. He's an expert at arm-twisting.'

That might be so, but Kelt didn't seem a man who'd yield to persuasion if he didn't want to. 'It's just as well he is,' she said crisply. 'The Tukuuluan government is pushed for money, so the school doesn't get much from them.'

Nodding, Kelt asked, 'Can I get you a drink? Wine? Something a little stronger? Or without alcohol?'

'Wine, thank you, if you have a light white.'

The wine he poured for her had a faint golden tinge, and the flavour was intense—a sensation-burst of freshness that almost persuaded her she was drinking champagne.

In spite of—or perhaps *because* of, she thought mordantly—being so acutely aware of him, she enjoyed Kelt's company. It was stimulating to match his incisive conversation, and a little to her surprise she discovered was he had a sense of humour. The half-hour or so before the meal went quickly.

Yet she had the feeling she was being tested, that for him the innocuous conversation was motivated by something more than social politeness. His hard eyes were always hooded, and she found herself weighing her words before she spoke.

That was worrying; she'd spent the past six years polishing a rather shallow, cheerful teacher persona that seemed to convince everyone she'd met.

Except this man. This man she was fiercely, *mindlessly* attracted to.

So, what was new? She'd felt lust before, and it had taken her into degradation and a never-ending fear that still kept her a prisoner in hiding.

And although there seemed to be a vast difference between her response to Felipe and her host for the evening, it was still lust. Better by far to ignore it—to pretend that she wasn't affected a bit by Kelt, that she didn't notice every tiny thing about him from the boldly arrogant lines of his profile to the easy grace of his movements. Even the sight of his lean, tanned hands on the white tablecloth over dinner sent shuddery little stabs of excitement through her.

Forget that night in Tukuulu. A cold shiver tightened her skin when she thought of what Felipe would do in the same situation. He'd take full advantage of her helplessness and vulnerability.

Kelt hadn't. And she had to respect him for that.

Dinner was served in a conservatory. Intoxicating perfume from the clusters of soft, creamy-pink flowers on a potted frangipani drifted through the room; Hani had always loved the fragrance, but here it seemed imbued with sensuous overtones she'd never noticed before.

But then, everything seemed suddenly more…more *more*, she thought, half-terrified at such foolishness. Colours seemed more luxurious, the food tasted sublime, and light gleamed off the glass and silverware with greater intensity. Just the sound of Kelt's voice produced a blooming of inner heat, a kind of nervous anticipation mixed with an excitement.

'Are you cold?' he asked.

'Not at all.'

Leaning back in his chair, he surveyed her through slightly narrowed eyes. 'You shivered.'

He saw too much. She said stiffly, 'It's nothing. Just some-one walking over my grave.'

To her astonishment he leaned forward and covered her hand. His was large and warm and relentless; when shock jerked her backwards his fingers closed around hers, holding her still.

'You *are* cold,' he said, those eyes narrowing further so that he was watching her through a screen of long black lashes.

Apprehension froze her into stillness. But he wasn't like Felipe, and his touch didn't repel her…

She swallowed and said in a constricted voice, 'I'm warm enough, thank you. Let me go.'

Although he released his grip his hard gaze didn't leave her face. 'I'll turn on some heat.'

Her eyes widened. However, one glance at his face told her there was no double meaning to his words.

'I don't need it. I'm perfectly comfortable,' she said curtly, her brows drawing together as she sent him a level glance that should have convinced him.

His brows drew together and he got to his feet. 'I'll be back in a moment.'

Before she could voice an objection he left the room.

Hani swallowed again. He was the most infuriatingly au-tocratic man—and she didn't want him watching her so closely that he noticed something as inconspicuous as the shiver that had started this. Some men were predators, hunters by nature, and although Kelt didn't show any signs of that, neither had Felipe at first.

Thrusting the vile memories back into the dark cupboard in her brain where she hid them, Hani waited tensely for Kelt to come back.

# CHAPTER FOUR

THE wrap Kelt brought into the conservatory matched the intense blue of lapis lazuli, and when he dropped it around Hani's shoulders it settled like a warm, light cloud. 'My cousin left it behind the last time she was here,' he said without moving. 'She won't mind you wearing it—she's the most generous person I know.'

Horrified by something that felt treacherously like a spark of jealousy, Hani said, 'I'll write her a note to thank her for the use of it.' Hairs lifted on the back of her neck, and she had to fight back an instinct to turn around and look up into his face.

'No need,' he said casually, walking away to sit down again. 'I'll tell her you were duly appreciative.'

Hani picked up her knife and fork and applied herself to the food on her plate, exasperated to find that the warmth of the pashmina was very welcome.

'Does Arthur cook all your meals?' she asked into the silence.

'He deals with dinner,' Kelt told her. 'I forage for myself when it comes to lunch and breakfast. As well as supervising the housekeeping and cooking, he likes to garden, and—as you discovered—he's a great fisherman.'

'He's a brilliant cook. This meal is superb.'

'Good. You need feeding up.'

Startled, she said forthrightly, 'That's hardly tactful.'

His answering smile was a masterpiece of irony. 'I'm not noted for my tact. And clearly you've lost weight while you've been ill.'

'I'm feeling much better,' she said defensively.

'You're still looking fragile. When I agreed that you could stay at the bach I was told the chances of you having another attack were pretty remote. However, you still have that delicate look. I'd prefer you to stay here rather than at the bach.'

He spoke as though he had the right to demand her agreement.

Hani's head came up and she stared incredulously at him. Fortunately her days of obeying men were over.

Fighting back a bewildering mixture of emotions—outrage at his high-handedness mingled with an odd warmth because he seemed to care about her welfare—she said evenly, 'That won't be necessary. I carry my medication with me all the time now, so any attack will be stopped before it has time to start.'

Although his expression didn't alter, she sensed a hardening in his attitude. 'Do you intend to stay inside the bach all the time?'

'Of course not, but I won't stray too far from it either.'

He said bluntly, 'No further than a hundred metres? Because that's about how far you were from the party when I found you, and by then you were incapable of moving. If no one had come along you'd have collapsed under the coconut palm you were clinging to.'

Her colour flared, but her eyes stayed steady when they met his. 'The circumstances were unusual.'

'In what way?' Clearly he didn't believe her.

'I knew during the speeches that I was getting an attack, but I stayed because in Tukuulu leaving while someone is making a speech is a huge insult.'

'Your cultural awareness does you credit.' The sardonic inflection in his tone flicked her on the raw. 'You must have realised you were letting yourself in for an attack of fever.'

'It's important to the Tukuuluans,' she retorted.

'Why didn't you get someone to help you to your cottage and make sure you got some medication into you?'

Lamely she admitted, 'I wasn't thinking straight by then. It won't happen again. Normally I just take medication and go to bed. When I wake up I'm fine.'

Heat burned across her cheekbones at the memory of waking and realising he'd changed her clothes. She didn't dare look at him in case he realised what she was thinking—and suspect that occasionally she fantasised guiltily about his hands on her skin, his gaze on her body...

He asked, 'What happens if you delay taking the medication?'

'I collapse, but the fever eventually passes,' she told him reluctantly.

'How long does that take?'

She parried his critical gaze with a level one of her own. Sorely tempted to gloss over the truth, she admitted, 'Quite some time.'

'You're being evasive.'

Her indignant glance made no impression on him. Meeting the burnished sheen of his gaze, she said belligerently, 'The first time I was in bed for almost a week.'

'How soon after the first symptoms do you need to take the drug?'

'The sooner the better.'

'How long, Hannah?'

Hani suspected that he'd continue interrogating her until she told him everything out of sheer exhaustion.

'Oh, about ten, fifteen minutes,' she flashed. 'But you needn't worry. I'm not going to collapse on the beach because—as I told you a few seconds ago—I take my medication with me all the time.'

He frowned. 'It's not good enough. You'd be much better off here where someone can keep an eye on you.'

For years Hani had managed to contain her naturally quick temper, but Kelt's ultimatum set a fuse to it. 'Have you any idea how arrogant you sound?' she demanded before she could bite the words back. 'You have no right—no right at all—to impose conditions on me. I can look after myself.'

'I might believe that if I hadn't *seen* the way you look after yourself,' he countered, startled by a swift stir of sensual appetite.

That serene façade she presented to the world was a sham, a mask to hide a much more animated personality. Her face was made for emotion—for laughter, for anger that came and went like summer lightning…for tenderness.

How would she look in the throes of passion?

His body responded with the now familiar need, hungry and reckless as wildfire. With lethal determination he reined it in, watching with half-closed eyes while she regained enough control to impose a rigid restraint over those mobile features. It was like watching a light being extinguished.

'All right,' she said shortly, 'I actually started to go, but the elders came in before I could. But I do not need cosseting or constant watching or checking. Think about it—*you'd* hate it. Why should I be any different?'

He lifted his brows, but said bluntly, 'I accept that, but I'd be a lot happier if you'd check in each day—say, in the evening.'

Would she recognise the classical negotiation gambit—make an outrageous demand, then offer a compromise? Kelt watched her face, almost sombre as she hesitated. What was she thinking?

Looking up with open challenge in those sultry eyes she said, 'And if I won't?'

He surveyed the lovely face opposite him, her sensuous mouth tightly controlled, and a rounded little chin held at an obstinate angle.

And she called *him* arrogant, he thought with hard amusement. Who exactly was she, and why was her crystalline English accent occasionally gentled by a soft slurring that somehow managed to sound piercingly erotic?

A woman of mystery in many ways—and obviously a fiercely independent one. He'd asked the principal about her background, and been surprised at how little his friend knew. She'd simply appeared one day at the school, offering to help in any way she could.

'Usually people who wash up in Tukuulu are on the run from something,' his friend had told him. 'Alcohol or drugs or the law or the media, or a romantic break-up that's convinced them their life is ruined. They think they can leave it all behind them and make a new start in the tropics, not realising that until they've faced it, everyone carries their past like a burden. People like that are no use to us.'

'But Hannah Court is.'

'Yes, we were lucky. She's great with the children. When we realised she had a talent for teaching she took every extramural course she could, and now she's a fully qualified infant teacher. Better still, she's got a small income from somewhere, so she can manage on the pittance we pay.'

'What nationality is she?'

His friend had looked a little self-conscious. 'I shouldn't be discussing her with you, but I assume she's English.'

'And you know nothing of her past or her circumstances?'

'She never speaks of them.'

'So she's a fugitive too.'

That was greeted by a shrug. 'Possibly. But she's not en-

cumbered by any obvious baggage. And she's kept a low
profile—no love affairs, no breakdowns, no binges. What
matters to us is that she fits really well into the island culture
and she's turned into a good, conscientious teacher.'

Naturally that was all that mattered to the principal of a
struggling school in the tropics, Kelt thought dryly now. But
it seemed a wicked waste for any woman as young and vibrant
as Hannah Court to hide away from the world. No love affairs
didn't, of course, mean she wasn't running from one that had
gone wrong. But after six years surely she'd have got over
such an experience.

That leashed awareness in Kelt stirred into life again.

He frowned, wondering why she intrigued him so much.
Partly it was masculine interest—even with the pallor of
illness she was lovely, her too slender body alluringly
curved, and from the way she'd curled into him he suspected she was no inexperienced virgin. And although he'd
learned to control his urges he had a normal man's needs
and hunger.

But this wasn't purely sexual.

From the first, even when he'd been sure she was either
drunk or stoned, he'd felt intensely protective towards her.
What the hell was she hiding from?

She'd blocked his every probe, either changing the subject
or simply ignoring his questions, so she was hiding *something*—and that something had to be pretty shattering.

Perhaps he should just let it go, but when he looked at her
he sensed a life wasted, a sorrow so deep she couldn't bear
to face it.

In Kelt's experience, the best thing to do with pain was
meet it head-on, accept it and deal with it, and then move on.

Kelt made up his mind. He'd use kidnapping as a last resort if she refused to compromise. 'If you won't agree to check in, I'll contact your principal.'

Her lovely face set into lines of mutiny. Common sense—and a strong sense of self-preservation—warned him that Hannah Court's past wasn't his business, and that he'd be foolish to tangle himself in her affairs. But he wasn't going to let her retreat to the bach without that promise.

Before she could say anything, he went on, 'And I want your word that you'll let me or Arthur know if you feel another attack coming on.'

Head held high, she met his steady gaze with cold composure. 'If it makes you feel happier I'll let someone know. And I'll ring the homestead every evening.' She added sweetly, 'Anything to please the man who is letting me live in his bach rent-free.'

Hani knew she sounded ungracious, but being backed into a corner made her feel wildly resentful. She'd feared Felipe's brutal domination, but at that age she'd been so sheltered she'd had no way of dealing with it. And then he'd made sure she couldn't escape it.

To be faced now with another dictatorial man angered her more than it frightened her—and that, she conceded reluctantly, was a relief.

'That's not an issue,' Kelt said shortly. 'Certainly not a personal one.'

'You can't actually stop me being grateful,' she snapped, 'but I won't bore you with it.'

'I don't want your damned gratitude!'

She opened her mouth to hurl an injudicious reply, then abruptly closed it before her intemperate words could burst forth. 'How did you do that? I never lose my temper!'

He stared at her, then gave a slow, wicked smile that sizzled through her defences, reducing her to silence.

But his tone was ironic when he said, 'Neither do I. As for how I managed to make you lose yours—according to my brother, a cousin and my grandmother,' he drawled, 'I suffer from a power complex.'

'They know you well.' She didn't try to hide the caustic note in her voice.

Kelt's raised eyebrow signified his understanding of her reluctance, but he appeared to take her surrender at face value, saying coolly, 'Thank you. I'll warn Arthur. He has a first-aid certificate and so do I.'

Irritated again, she blurted, 'I won't *need* first aid—well, not unless I fall off a cliff. I'm perfectly capable of looking after myself.'

There was a moment's silence until he said with silky clarity, 'I hope you don't intend to renege. I really don't like people who lie.'

Then he'd *hate* her—her whole life was built on lies. She said unevenly, 'You're just going to have to trust me.'

He held her gaze, then nodded and stretched out his hand. 'So shake on it.'

She should be getting accustomed to the way his touch burned through her, but it seemed to be getting more and more potent.

Fighting a sensuous weakness as they shook hands, she managed to produce something that resembled a smile. 'I'm sorry, I'm being dull company, but I have to confess to getting tired very early in the evening.'

As she knew he would, he examined her face with that analytical gaze before getting to his feet. 'Far from dull. In fact, the more I know of you the more interesting I find you,' he said ambiguously, 'but I'll take you home.'

His instant agreement should have pleased her. Instead it made her feel as though she'd been rejected. *Idiot*, she scolded herself fiercely and went to put down the pretty shawl.

Kelt said, 'Keep it on. It will be cool outside now, and you'll need it.'

Arthur saw them out, his face crinkling with restrained pleasure when she said, 'That was a superb meal, thank you.'

'My pleasure, miss,' he said with a half-bow.

Kelt was right; the air was much crisper than it had been before sunset, and Hani had to bite her lips to stop them trembling. Snuggling into the shawl in Kelt's big Range Rover, she realised that if she wanted to be comfortable for the next three months she'd have to buy new clothes.

She fought back a twinge of panic. Her trust fund—a secret between them, her godmother had told her with a wink when she revealed its existence on her seventeenth birthday, because every woman needed money she didn't have to account for— provided her with a small income, but it wasn't enough to stretch to clothes she'd never wear again.

Perhaps there was a secondhand shop in a nearby town.

'What's the matter?' Kelt asked as they went over the cattle grid onto the road that led to the bach.

He must be able to read her like a book. Forcing her brows back into their normal place, she said airily, 'I was just thinking I need new clothes. I know it's summer, but I'm used to tropical heat.'

'There are a couple of quite good boutiques in Kaitake, our service centre,' he told her. 'Unless you need the clothes urgently I'll take you there the day after tomorrow. I'm going there on business, and you can have a look around.'

Boutiques she didn't need—too expensive. 'I could walk—'

'No, it's not the local village—that's Waituna, and it's

about five kilometres north, but it's just a small general store and a petrol station. Kaitake is on the coast about twenty minutes' drive away.'

'I see.' After a moment's hesitation she said formally, 'Thank you, that's very kind of you.'

He shrugged. 'You'll find the copy of the road code I promised you in the glove pocket.'

Back at the homestead, Kelt strolled into the kitchen and got himself a glass of water, looking up as Arthur came in through the door that led to his own quarters.

'Tell me, Arthur, what part of the UK does Miss Court come from?'

'She's not English,' Arthur said promptly and decisively.

Kelt lifted an enquiring eyebrow. 'She sounds very English.'

'Not to me. She speaks it superbly, but I'd wager quite a lot of money that English is not her first language.' He frowned and said slowly, 'In fact, I think I detect hints of a Creole heritage.'

'Caribbean?' Interest quickened through Kelt. He set the glass down on the bench.

'Could be,' Arthur said slowly, frowning, 'but I doubt it. I just don't know—but I'm certain she's not English.'

During the night Hani woke from a deep, deep sleep and heard rain quietly falling onto the roof, and in the morning everything outside glittered in the sunlight as though dusted with diamonds.

The water in the bay was a little discoloured, and when she went for a walk after breakfast she discovered one side of the small stream had fallen in, the clay damming the stream so that it backed up and was already oozing up to the farm road.

Back at the bach she rang through to the homestead. And was *not*, she told herself stoutly, disappointed when Arthur answered.

'Right, I'll make sure the farm manager hears about it,' he said. 'Thank you very much for reporting it, Miss Court.'

Later in the day she walked back along the road and came upon someone clearing the stream. One of the huge trees hung over the water there, its leaves sifting the sunlight so that it fell in dapples of golden light across the man in the water.

Kelt, she thought, her heart soaring exultantly.

He'd taken off his shirt, and the sun played across the powerful muscles of his bronze shoulders and back. An urgent heat flamed in the pit of her stomach as her eyes lingered on each powerful thrust of his arms as when he dug through the temporary dam with fluid strength, tossing shovelfuls of clay back up the bank.

Her response shocked her—a wild rush of adrenalin, of heady anticipation, a swift, unspoken recognition in the very deepest levels of her heart and mind.

As if her passionate claiming had somehow sent out subliminal signals, Kelt looked up. His tanned face showed a flash of white as he smiled, but his gaze was coolly assessing.

Without altering the steady, smooth rhythm of his shovelling, he said, 'Good morning.'

'Good morning,' Hani replied sedately, hoping her voice sounded as impersonal as his. Triumphantly she fished in her pocket and held out a container of pill capsules.

His smile reappeared. 'Good girl.'

Reaching up to a low branch, he used it to swing himself up onto the bank. With a smile that turned her sizzling appreciation into a flame, pure and keen and intense, he said, 'And thanks for being a good citizen and reporting the blockage in the creek.'

'It looked as though it might wash out the road.' Hani felt shy and foolish, the urgent instructions of her mind at war with the eager pleading of her body.

'It could have.' He turned and surveyed his handiwork. He'd opened enough of a breach for the discoloured water to start flowing sluggishly out onto the beach. 'Once I took over Kiwinui I started a programme of fencing the gullies and riversides off from stock and planting them up with native plants. This land erodes badly if it's not cared for, and the farm manager who ran it when I was under age cared more for production than for conservation.' He shrugged. 'He was a man of his time.'

Hani nodded. After her father's death Rafiq had introduced a variety of conservation measures to Moraze, somewhat to the astonishment and dismay of many of his subjects. 'How do you stop the bank from eroding?'

He indicated a tray of small plants on the tray of a small truck. 'We run a nursery where we grow seeds from the native plants on the station. Our native flax loves wet feet, and is extremely good at holding up banks. As well, this summer the road to the bach is being moved further up the hill so that it's not running across a natural wetlands area.'

'Are you going to plant those little seedlings?' she asked.

'Once I've finished clearing this away, yes.'

Impetuously Hani said, 'I'll help.'

His brows shot up. 'You'll get dirty.'

She shrugged. 'So? I've been dirty before, and as far as I know it all washed off.'

'You haven't got gumboots.'

'I can go barefoot,' she told him, exasperated by his obvious image of her as a useless creature. She sat down and slid her feet out of her elderly sneakers, aware that Kelt stood and watched her.

When she stood up again he said, 'Do you know how to plant things?'

'I'm not an expert,' she said, sending him a look that held more challenge than was probably wise, 'but if you tell me what you want me to do and where the plants should go, I'm sure I can cope.'

Still with that infuriating air of amusement he did, digging holes for the plants, then going back to clean up the sides of the stream while she planted, patting the earth around each little flax bush with care.

They didn't talk much, although she learned that in this part of New Zealand there were no streams, only creeks. And although she was still acutely, heatedly aware of him, she found the silence and the work oddly companionable, even soothing.

Well, soothing if she kept her eyes on the plants and didn't let them stray to Kelt, she thought mordantly, lowering her lashes after a peek at the smooth sheen of his skin when he threw another shovelful of clay up onto the bank.

'There,' she said when she'd finished.

Two long strides brought him up beside her. 'Well done.' He paused, and into the silence fell a sweet, echoing peal of birdsong. 'A tui,' he told her laconically, pointing out a black bird, sheened with green and bronze and with a bobble of white feathers at the throat. 'They visit the flax flowers to get nectar.'

She eyed the tall, candelabra-like stalks that held wine-coloured flowers. The bird sank its beak into the throat of another one, then climbed to the top of the stalk and, as if in thanks, lifted its head and sang again, its notes pealing out like the chime of small silver bells into the warm, sea-scented air.

Sheer delight prompted Hani to murmur, 'It's just—so beautiful here.'

There was another silence before he said, 'Indeed it is.'

Something in his tone made her glance up.

He was looking at her, not at the tui, and deep inside her desire burned away the warnings of her mind so that they crumbled into ashes. Hani forgot she had muddy hands and feet; she'd wiped sweat off her face and there was probably mud there too.

Under his hooded scrutiny her lips and throat went dry. Tension arced between them like lightning.

*Get out of here*, she thought frantically, *before you do something stupid, like tilt your head towards him.* She fought back an imperative desire to do just that and find out once and for all what Kelt's kiss would feel like.

As though he sensed her desperate effort to keep calm, she saw him impose control, his eyes darken, and the dangerous moment passed.

Yet he'd wanted her…

Nothing, she thought with a flash of pure rapture, could ever take that away. But far more wondrous was that *she* wanted *him*. After six years of being sure Felipe had killed that part of her, she felt passion and desire again.

Kelt said, 'And it will be even more beautiful when these plants grow. Thank you. Kiwinui will always have some part of you here.'

Unexpectedly touched by the thought, she said, 'I enjoyed doing it.'

'I just hope it doesn't make you feel worse. Remember, any shiver, anything that worries you, ring the homestead.' He glanced at his watch. 'I'm afraid I have to go—I'm expecting a call from overseas.'

Back at the bach she told herself she should be grateful to that unknown person who was calling him long-distance.

Falling in lust with Kelt was one thing, but her headstrong desire to know him far more intimately was a much more dangerous development.

# CHAPTER FIVE

WHEN she rang that night, Arthur answered again. He enquired after her health, said Kelt had told him she'd helped plant the flax and hoped her hard work hadn't made her condition worse.

'No, I'm very well, thank you,' she replied politely. After she'd rung off she thought sombrely that Kelt was probably out with some local beauty.

Trying to laugh herself out of that foolish mood didn't work, so she went to bed and dreamed of him, only to wake cross and crumpled in the big bed the next morning.

'Enough,' she told her reflection severely as she applied moisturiser. 'OK, so you think he's gorgeous. No, let's be embarrassingly honest here—you want to go to bed with him. Very, very much.'

And even more since she'd seen him clearing the stream—*creek*, she amended hurriedly—shirtless, his bronzed torso exposed in lethal power and forceful energy.

Her breath caught in her throat. Hurriedly she finished the rest of her morning regime, telling herself sternly, 'But even if he feels the same way, there's absolutely no future for this. In three months' time you're going back to Tukuulu, where you're safe.'

And she'd never be able to forge any sort of future with him—or any man, not so long as Felipe was alive.

But Felipe hadn't found her, she thought, stopping and staring sightlessly into the mirror. And here, in New Zealand, she felt just as safe as she had in Tukuulu.

Perhaps there was a chance...

'Forget it!' she said curtly. 'It's not going to happen, not now, not ever.'

So Kelt had moments when he wanted her. Big deal; for most men that meant very little. If she allowed herself to surrender to the erotic charge between them, he'd probably enjoy an affair, then wave her goodbye at that tiny airport without anything more than mild regret.

Or—even more cringe-making—perhaps he hadn't liked what he'd seen when he'd taken off her wet dress and slipped the shift over her head...

Whatever, an affair was out! So when he arrived in a few minutes she'd be cool and dismissive and completely ignore the chemistry between them.

Dead on time he drove down the track. He was already out of the vehicle when Hani walked out to meet him, her heartbeat racing into an erratic tattoo. Lean and lithe and very big, he surveyed her with an intimidating scrutiny for several seconds before his smile not only melted her bones but also set her wayward pulse off into the stratosphere.

Dizzily she said, 'Good morning,' in her most guarded voice.

Until he'd smiled at her she'd been very aware that this day was considerably cooler than the previous one. Now however, she felt almost feverish.

His gaze hardened. 'You're looking a bit tired.'

'I'm fine,' she said quickly, dismissively.

A glance at the sedan he'd driven made her fight back a

gurgle of laughter. He so did *not* look like that four-cylinder, family-style vehicle! No, he should be driving something wickedly male and dangerous…

So what did it mean that he thought this sedate vehicle suitable for her?

Nothing, she reminded herself staunchly; don't go reading symbolism into everything he does. He was extremely kind to offer what was probably his only spare vehicle; that it happened to be a reliable, boring car was all to the good!

Now, if only she could satisfy him that the past few hours spent devouring the contents of the road code had turned her into a fit driver for New Zealand roads.

'Hop behind the wheel,' Kelt said, making it sound rather too much of an order.

With a touch of asperity Hani said, 'Thank you,' and climbed into the car. Once there, she spent time familiarising herself with the instrument panel.

Kelt got in beside her, immediately sucking all of the air out of the interior.

'Ah, an automatic,' she said, memories of being taught to drive flooding her. 'My brother used to say…'

Appalled, she bit back the rest of the comment, hoping desperately that he hadn't heard her.

Not a chance.

'Your brother used to say—?'

Bending forward, she hid her face by groping for the lever that moved the seat. 'That they're for old ladies of both sexes.'

'I wonder if he'd feel the same once he'd driven on some of Northland's roads,' Kelt said dryly.

'Perhaps not.' Her shaking fingers closed on the lever, but

she was so tense she misjudged the effort needed, and the seat jerked forward. However, the several moments spent adjusting it to her liking gave her precious time to compose herself.

Straightening, she said in her most cheerful tone, 'That's better—I can reach the pedals now. Not everybody has such long legs as you.'

'I wouldn't call yours short.'

An equivocal note beneath the amused words brought colour to her cheeks, but at least she'd diverted the conversation away from Rafiq. 'They certainly aren't in the same league as yours,' she said brightly, and put the car into gear.

On Tukuulu she'd sometimes driven the school's elderly four-wheel-drive, wrestling with gears that stuck, barely functioning brakes and an engine that had to be coaxed, so this well-maintained car was no problem. Nevertheless she drove cautiously, keeping the speed down; the farm road might also be well-maintained, but it wasn't sealed, and the gravel surface was a challenge.

Showing an unexpected understanding, Kelt stayed silent while she found her own way around the instruments and got the feel of the vehicle. By the time she'd taken them past the cluster of workers' cottages and big sheds, she was feeling quite at home behind the wheel, but at the junction with the sealed road she braked, and looked sideways at Kelt.

Eyes half-hidden by thick lashes, he said coolly, 'You're an excellent driver, as I'm sure you know. Your brother taught you well.'

Hoping he didn't notice the sudden whiteness of her knuckles, she loosened her grip on the wheel. 'Do you want to take over now?'

'No. There's not another car in sight. The speed limit's a hundred kilometres an hour.'

'Not on this road, surely,' she muttered, loosening her hold on the wheel to steer out.

'Officially yes, but you're right—most of the time it's safer to stick to eighty. Some of the corners aren't well-cambered.'

Oddly enough, his presence beside her lent Hani confidence. There wasn't much traffic, although she found the frequent huge trucks intimidating.

'It's the main highway north,' he said when she voiced her surprise at the number. 'The railway doesn't come this far, so everything is transported by truck.'

One day, she thought, she'd like to be a passenger and really check out the countryside. She'd seen nothing on that night drive from the airport with Arthur, and her occasional sideways glance revealed a landscape of dramatically bold hills and lush valleys.

'Take the left turn at the next intersection,' Kelt instructed after a few minutes.

It delivered them to a small town situated on an estuary. Shaded by palms and bright with flowers and subtropical vegetation, it looked prosperous and charming. Not even the mangroves that clogged the riverbank could give it a sinister air.

'Kaitake,' Kelt told her. 'Turn right here and then a left into the car park.'

He waited until she'd switched off the engine before saying, 'I'll meet you here at twelve-thirty. That should give you time to have a good look at several of the boutiques before I buy you lunch.'

'You don't have to buy me lunch,' she protested, firmly squelching a forbidden spurt of pleasure and anticipation.

'You drove me here,' he said, not giving an inch. 'One good turn deserves another.'

He stopped any further objection by removing himself

from the car and coming around to open her door. Baulked, Hani grabbed her bag and got out, taking a deep breath.

'That's not so. I'd like to buy you lunch,' she said crisply, looking up into his hard, handsome face.

Bad move; once more her pulses ratcheted up and that odd weakness softened her bones. She had to suck in a rapid breath and steady her voice before she could go on. 'You're lending me the car and, although lunch seems a pretty poor recompense for your kindness, it's the least I can do.'

'The car would be idle if you weren't using it. Are you always so fiercely independent?'

Independence kept her safe. She shrugged, her mouth tightening. 'Yes,' she said in a deliberately offhanded voice.

That disbelieving brow lifted. 'Very well, you can buy me lunch. By now you must know I have a hearty appetite.'

And possibly not just for food... The sexy little thought popped into her head as she forced herself to say airily, 'That's no problem.'

Of course he ate well—he was a big man—but he also exuded a prowling sensuality that probably meant he was an extremely good lover as well.

And no doubt there were plenty of women who responded to that magnetic, masculine charisma. Plenty of women had wanted to go to bed with Felipe—a situation he used with cynical disregard for them. Would Kelt?

She tried to relax her tight muscles. Forget Felipe; it had been sheer bad luck—and her own trusting foolishness—that the first man she'd fallen for had been a career criminal who'd seen her as a means to an end.

'Is something the matter?'

Kelt's voice, forceful and uncompromising, jolted her back to the present.

'I—no, no, of course not,' she said quickly and, hoping to deflect his attention, she went on with a brightness she hoped didn't sound too brittle, 'Nothing could possibly be wrong— I'm about to buy some clothes!'

His unyielding blue gaze held hers a second longer before his mouth curved into a smile that sent a sizzle of excitement through her, one that burned away all her sensible decisions and left her open and exposed to this wildfire hunger, this sensuous craving that was trying to take her over.

He startled her by taking her elbow. At the touch of his hand—strong and purposeful—Hani tensed. Dry-mouthed, she sent him an anxious glance, only relaxing when she saw his calm expression. Swallowing, she concentrated on putting her feet down precisely, every cell in her body taut and alert.

Yet in spite of his closeness and that light grip on her elbow, no panic kicked beneath her ribs; in fact, she thought worriedly, she felt oddly protected and safe.

And that was really, really dangerous.

Talk! she commanded herself.

Aloud she said brightly, 'I didn't expect to see verandas out over the streets in New Zealand. It gives the place a very tropical look.'

'Our sun's not as hot as it is in the tropics, but we live beneath a hole in the ozone layer,' Kelt told her, 'and it can rain just as heavily here as it does there.'

'It's so…fresh.'

'If you're comparing it to Tukuulu, industrial areas aren't noted for their beauty and freshness,' he observed on a dry note.

Several passers-by greeted him, their gazes coming in-evitably to rest on her. She felt too conspicuous, their interest setting her nerves on edge. Kelt's compelling combination of raw male charisma and formidable authority would always attract attention, she thought with a hint of panic. So she wouldn't come here again with him.

Uncannily detecting her unease, he glanced down at her. 'What is it?'

Hani said the first thing that came into her mind. 'You promised me boutiques. I can't see any here.'

'There's one about a hundred metres from here, and another just around the corner.' That far too perceptive gaze swept her face. 'You're sure you're all right?'

'I'm fine,' she said, and tried out her best smile, sweetly persuasive.

It failed entirely; if anything, his eyes hardened and his voice turned caustic. 'Stop playing games with me.'

'I will when you stop being so—so mother-hennish,' she retorted, chagrined because he'd seen through her so easily. 'If it helps you to stop fussing, I'll agree that the doctor at Tukuulu was right; I did need a holiday in a cooler place. Since I've been here I've been sleeping like a log, and my appetite's come back. And I feel more energetic. I don't need to be watched and monitored and scrutinised as though I'm going to faint any minute.'

His survey didn't soften, but his mouth quirked. 'Is that what I was doing?'

'That's what it felt like,' she said, startled to realise that, as much as his concern irked her, it satisfied something she'd been unaware of—a debilitating need to be cared for. Her colleagues were kind and helpful and friendly, but they had their own lives, their own affairs to worry about. The friendships she'd formed at the school were genuine, but she'd deliberately kept them superficial.

A voice from behind cooed Kelt's name. Hani's heart clamped when she saw the woman who'd caught them up.

Hardly more than a girl, the newcomer was stunning. Hair an artful shade of auburn, her eyes huge and golden-brown in a beautiful, cleverly made-up face, she looked like sunshine and laughter and innocence, her curvy little body emphasised by clothes that hadn't been bought in any small town.

Her radiance made Hani feel old and tired and depraved, her past cutting her off from such exuberant, joyous youthfulness.

'Kelt, you're the tallest man around. I saw you from the other end of the street,' the newcomer said, beaming at him. She turned to Hani, and her smile widened. 'Hello, you must be the new guest in the bach. How are you liking it?'

'Very much, thank you,' Hani said politely.

In a neutral voice Kelt said, 'Hannah, this is my cousin, Rosemary Matthews.'

'Rosie,' Kelt's cousin said with an admonitory gaze at him. She shook hands with vigour, and added cheerfully, 'No one ever calls me Rosemary. And just between you and me, our relationship is more *whanau* than cousin—so distant it doesn't count.' Her smile turned wicked. 'Consider me one of the aspirants for Kelt's hand.'

Hani's social smile turned into a startled laugh. She glanced up at Kelt, who was studying his cousin with a mixture of austerity and amusement, and asked involuntarily, 'One of the aspirants? How many are there?'

'Dozens,' Rosie told her without any sign of embarrassment, 'if not *hundreds*—they come full of hope, and they go away broken-hearted. I spend quite a lot of time patting shoulders and supplying tissues to weeping women who've realised they don't have a chance.' She heaved a theatrical sigh. 'My heart bleeds for them, but I have to be strong so I can plead my own case.'

'Stop teasing,' Kelt said indulgently. 'Hannah might just take you seriously.'

'She seems far too sensible to do that,' Rosie returned, eyes sparkling with impudence. But when she transferred her gaze back to Hani some of the laughter went from her face. 'Have we met before? I seem to know you—and yet I don't think we've been introduced, have we?'

Of all the people to induce that frantic kick of panic beneath Hani's ribs, this sunshiny girl was the last she'd have imagined. She shook her head and steadied her voice to say, 'This is my first visit to New Zealand.'

Kelt said briefly, 'Hannah lives in Tukuulu—in the islands. She's been ill and needs to recuperate in a cooler climate. What are you doing here? I thought you were going to Auckland with your mother.'

She shrugged. 'I decided not to go—she's off to the opera with the new boyfriend, and you know, tubby little tenors angsting in high Cs at shrieking ladies with huge bosoms are *so* not my thing.' She looked from one to the other. 'Are you going to lunch, because if you are can I come too?'

Amused, Hani glanced at Kelt, who was scanning that vivid little face with a certain grimness.

'No,' he said calmly. 'Hannah needs rest, and you are not restful.'

Hani blinked. He sent her a silent, don't-get-mixed-up-in-this warning.

Mournfully Rosie responded, 'I'll take that as a compliment. Of course, I could just keep quiet and enjoy the ambience.'

'Quiet? You?' Kelt asked, his dry tone not quite hiding his affection. 'Go on—catch up with the friend I can see waiting for you outside the café.'

Rosie gave a wounded sigh, rapidly followed by another of those infectious smiles. 'I try so hard to outwit him,' she confided to Hani, 'but he sees through me every time. It's been nice talking to you—we must get together when you feel up to being stimulated! Although quite frankly, I think Kelt is more than enough excitement for any woman, let alone one who's convalescing!'

With a saucy glance at her cousin, she set off down the street, hips swaying seductively, the sun burnishing her superbly cut hair to copper.

Kelt said dryly, 'She's nowhere near so ingenuous as she seems, but there's no harm in her.'

'She's very forthright,' Hani ventured cautiously, adding because her words seemed like criticism, 'but I imagine she's great fun.'

'She has an interesting sense of humour,' he conceded, checking his watch. 'All right, I'll see you back at the car park. Have fun shopping.'

Hani nodded and walked sedately towards the boutique he'd mentioned, wondering whether his cousin would be lying in wait somewhere. However, there wasn't a sign of her anywhere in the busy street. And one glance at the boutique window told her she couldn't afford anything it sold, but in case Kelt was still able to see her she went inside.

She'd been right. The racks were full of clothes she'd love to buy, but not at those prices. Possibly Rosie had bought some of her outfit here after all.

The quick interplay between the cousins and their obvious affection for each other made her sadly envious. Or enviously sad... Rafiq had been her adored big brother, but he was quite a bit older and their relationship had become less close after their parents had died and he'd had to rule Moraze.

Oh, she'd always known he loved her, but there wasn't the easy camaraderie she'd seen between Kelt and Rosie. And those few minutes in their company had shown her another side of the man she found so dangerously interesting; they convinced her that her instinctive trust of him was justified.

After a quick, regretful smile at the saleswoman she left, resigned to the same experience in the next shop. That wasn't so upmarket, but still too expensive.

Finally she tracked down a secondhand shop in one of the back streets, between a pet shop and an internet café.

Ignoring the delectable puppies tumbling around in the window, she hurried inside the charity shop, and to her relief found exactly what she wanted—several light tops, a pair of sleek black trousers in a very fine woollen fabric, a pair of jeans and two merino-wool jerseys, all good chain-store quality.

'Are you going off on holiday to the northern hemisphere?' the woman behind the counter asked as Hani examined herself in the one big mirror in the shop.

Hani said, 'That would be lovely, but no, I've been living in a warmer climate.'

'They could have been made for you,' the woman said, inspecting the well-cut trousers and a feather-soft merino jersey in a soft peach that lent a golden gleam to Hani's skin. 'Look, if you're cold, why don't you wear them away? They've all been washed and dry-cleaned. I'll pack your own clothes in with the other ones you've bought.'

New Zealanders—well, the ones she'd met, Hani thought wryly as she walked out—were a helpful lot. On the street she checked her watch, allowing herself another wistful glance at the puppies before she hurried to the car park.

Kelt was waiting, not impatiently but as though no one had ever been late for him. He turned as she came towards him, and once more she saw that gleam in his eyes, a hooded glitter of appreciation.

Something strange and dramatic happened to her heart;

it seemed to soar within her, and she was filled by breath-less anticipation, as though the world was full of wonderful possibilities.

After a swift scrutiny Kelt said, 'You look stunning.'

'I— Thank you.' Too breathless to go on, she groped for the keys she'd dropped into her bag. 'I'll just put my purchases in the car.'

'Do you want to drive again?'

Keys in hand, she looked up at him, his tanned face angular, his expression controlled. 'Aren't we eating here?'

'There's a very good restaurant in a vineyard not far away.'

Too late now to hope it wasn't expensive. She'd thought they'd eat at a café. Abandoning caution, she said, 'I might as well get as much experience as I can while you're here to ride shotgun. I still haven't quite got my bearings.'

'You don't need anyone to oversee your driving.'

'Thank you,' she said, the warmth of his comment lasting until they reached the vineyard in the hills a few kilometres from town.

'It could almost be some part of Tuscany,' she observed when they were seated on the wide terrace beneath a canopy of hot-pink bougainvillea flowers. It overlooked a small valley filled by a body of water too big to be called a pond, too small for a lake.

Kelt asked idly, 'Have you been there?'

She'd spent a holiday with a school friend in a magnificent villa in the heart of Tuscany. 'I've seen a lot of photographs,' she returned, hating the fact that she'd fudged. Still, she might be implying something that wasn't true, but at least she hadn't come out with a direct lie.

Perhaps something in her tone alerted him, because he sub-jected her to another of those coolly judicial looks. She was prickly with embarrassment when he said, 'A glass of wine?'

'No, thanks.' She gave a rueful little smile. 'I tend to drift off to sleep if I drink in the daytime. Not a good look over the lunch table, or behind the wheel.'

'Not a good look in most places.' A note of reservation in his voice made her wonder whether he was remembering the night she'd collapsed in his arms.

They'd felt so good...

Heat touched her cheeks; she bent her head and applied herself to the menu.

Which, she noted with a sinking heart, had no prices. In her experience that meant the food was astronomically expensive. Well, she'd insisted on paying; no matter how much it cost she'd manage. Thrift was something she'd learned over the past years.

Clearly Kelt was well-known; the woman who'd shown them to their table had greeted him with a warm smile and by his first name. She was too professional to make her curiosity about Hani obvious.

Kelt ordered a beer for himself and freshly squeezed lime juice with soda for her, before saying, 'It looks as though you had a satisfactory morning shopping for clothes.'

'Thank you,' she said politely, adding, 'Is Rosie the cousin who owns that shawl?'

'Yes.' A strand of golden sunlight probed through the leafy canopy over the terrace, summoning a lick of fire from his hair.

A fierce, sweet sensation burst through her, startling her with its intensity. After her treatment by Felipe she'd never thought to experience desire again—in fact, she'd welcomed her total lack of interest in the opposite sex because it kept her safe.

But this was desire as she'd never known it—a cell-deep hunger that pierced her with helpless delight. And with fear. She didn't dare fall in love again.

But she could perhaps exorcise Felipe's malign influence over her life by—

By what? An affair…

Shocked yet fascinated by this outrageous thought, she said in her most sedate tone, 'Then I must write her that note to thank her.'

'Oh, you'll see her again. She's as curious as a cat. In a few days she'll be down at the bach trying to lure you out of your solitude.'

Rosie was a nice, neutral topic. Relieved, Hani seized on it. 'What does she do? Is she at university?'

'Gap year,' he said succinctly. 'Her mother decided she was too immature to be let loose on an unsuspecting world, so she's staying at home.'

Something in his voice made her say, 'You don't approve.'

'I think she should be doing something, not just swanning around having fun,' he said uncompromisingly. 'She's got a damned good brain beneath that red hair, and she needs to exercise it instead of wasting time flitting from party to party.'

'Perhaps she needs a year of enjoying herself. High school is hard work.'

'She's never had to work hard for anything.' He dismissed the subject of his cousin. 'So tell me what you're planning to do while you're here.'

A mischievous impulse persuaded her to say, 'I haven't decided yet. Perhaps I'll do some running around too.'

He cocked that brow at her. 'It shouldn't do you any harm, although you're still looking a bit fine-drawn.'

His tone was impersonal, but a note in it fanned the forbidden, smouldering flame inside her. Ignoring it she said steadily, 'Actually, I'm not the flitting type.'

'Are you going to be able to go back to the tropics?'

Startled, she said, 'Of course. This is the twenty-first century, not the nineteenth.' She lifted her glass of lime juice. 'Here's to the miracles of modern medicine.'

'I'll drink to that,' he said, and did so.

As he set his glass down Hani looked out across the valley and said, 'The vines look like braids across the hillside. They must be stunning in the autumn when the leaves change colour.'

'We don't get intense autumn colours this far north,' Kelt told her. 'For those you need to go to the South Island.'

He'd moved slightly so that his back was presented to a group just being seated, and she wondered if he was ashamed of being seen with her. These women seemed overdressed for a casual vineyard lunch, but their clothes—like Rosie's—bore the discreet indications of skilful design and obvious expense.

Kelt might be a snob—she hadn't seen him with other people enough to know otherwise—but his enviable aura of self-assurance surely meant any embarrassment was unlikely.

He'd certainly shrugged off his *distant* cousin's open claim to him—not to mention her statement that women wept when they realised he wasn't interested in them. And without so much as a tinge of colour along those sweeping, stark cheekbones. Perhaps it was a joke between them?

A comment from Kelt broke into her anxious thoughts. 'That's an interesting expression.'

Hani was saved from answering by the arrival of the first course—iced soup for her, a considerably more substantial dish for him.

As she tackled the soup she thought ironically that she hadn't eaten with a man for over six years, and here she was, for the second time in two days, sharing a meal with the most interesting man she'd ever met.

And one of the best-looking. Apart from Rafiq, she thought loyally, but of course her brother didn't affect her like—

Her thoughts came to a jarring halt.

Well, OK, she *was* affected by Kelt.

But only physically. She was safe from the shattering emotional betrayal she'd suffered at Felipe's hands.

Kelt had shown her he wasn't at all like Felipe—that lick of contempt in his voice when he'd asked if she was drunk or drugged, his affection for his cousin, the children's innocent, open respect and liking…

Any woman who took him for a lover wouldn't end up with splintered self-esteem and a death wish.

And she'd learned a lot in six years, grown up, become a different woman from the child-adult who'd fallen headlong for Felipe's false charm. Even then, it hadn't taken her too long to realise she'd fallen in love with a carefully constructed image, a mirage.

A trap.

And if she wanted to free herself from the lingering after-effects of her experience with Felipe, prove that she was able to handle a mature relationship, then Kelt would be the ideal lover. Miraculously he'd woken the long-dead part of her that was able to respond.

And he wanted her…

Common sense did its best to squelch the secret thrill of excitement, warning Hani not to allow herself the forbidden luxury of impossible dreams. Nothing had really changed; as long as Felipe was alive she'd never be safe, and neither was anyone else she knew.

# CHAPTER SIX

KELT'S voice—aloof, rather cool—broke into Hani's tumbled thoughts. 'Don't you like that soup? I can order something else for you if you'd rather.'

'No, it's delicious, thank you.' Startled, she drank some more without tasting it. She was not going to let herself fantasise about an affair with him—it was altogether too dangerous. Reining in her too vivid imagination, she said sedately, 'They have a great chef.'

'She's an American woman with a Brazilian background who met her New Zealand husband in London. When he decided to come back here and grow grapes she set up the restaurant. It's becoming rather famous.'

'I can understand why,' she said, suddenly longing for the potent chilli dishes of her homeland.

A large dog of indeterminate breed wandered around the corner, accompanied by an entourage of ducks. They parted ways, the ducks heading downhill to the pond, the dog stopping to survey the diners. After a few seconds of sniffing, it headed for Hani.

'Shall I send him away?' Kelt said. 'He's well-behaved and very much a part of the restaurant, but if you're wary of dogs he can look intimidating.'

'I like dogs.' Quelling a bitter memory, she held out her hand, back upwards, so that the dog could scent her. It obliged delicately, and with excellent manners refrained from actually landing the automatic lick on her skin.

'Yes, you're a handsome creature,' Hani said softly. 'What's your name?'

Kelt waved away a waiter who'd started towards them. 'Rogue. And he's not allowed to beg.'

'He's not begging, are you, Rogue?'

A woman called from behind a screen, and obediently Rogue bounded off.

'I can see you know how to deal with dogs,' Kelt remarked.

'I grew up with them,' she said simply.

Felipe had bought her a puppy. She'd learned to love it—and then, a month or so later, they'd quarrelled.

She'd gone out, and when she'd got home the puppy was dead. He'd got one of his servants to drown it. To teach her a lesson, he'd said and, when she'd wept, told her negligently that because she'd learned that lesson he'd buy her another one.

That was when Hani had realised that to him she was every bit as expendable as the puppy—something he'd bought, something he could order to be killed just to make a point…

Her throat closed; she swallowed and smiled and said much more brightly, 'I wonder what interesting mix of bloodlines led to Rogue's conformation.'

'German Shepherd, certainly, and perhaps a hint of bull terrier—with border collie? Apart from that, who knows?'

The shutters had come down again, barring him from her thoughts. Kelt's eyes narrowed as he surveyed her calm, emotionless face. Hannah Court's stubborn refusal to give him any information about herself was getting to him.

She was nothing like the women he usually wanted. After

an experience when he was young and callow enough to break a woman's heart he'd been careful to choose lovers as sophisticated as he was. He'd given up expecting to fall in love—and he had no intention of falling in love with Hannah Court either.

But she was an intriguing mystery, one he wanted to solve. He hadn't missed the moment of stiffness when Rosie had suggested she might have seen her before. She wore that disciplined composure like armour, yet flashes of tension broke through it—when he touched her, when she'd inadvertently revealed she had a brother.

He doubted that she'd been involved in anything criminal, but possibly her six years in the mining wasteland of Tukuulu was self-punishment. Was she expiating some sin?

Or was she afraid?

She hadn't pulled away when he'd touched her—she'd actually flinched, as though expecting pain. A violent surge of outrage took him completely by surprise; he had to stop his hand from clenching into a fist beside his plate.

Hani looked up at him, those dark eyes green and unreadable even though she was smiling. 'Probably a couple of other breeds too,' she said. 'I'm glad Rogue's well looked after. People shouldn't have dogs if they aren't prepared to love them.'

Kelt heard the momentary hesitation, the flicker of grief in her voice, and watched with narrowed eyes as she scrambled to her feet and said, 'If you'll just excuse me...'

Without waiting for a response she headed across the terrace and into the restaurant.

What the hell had precipitated that? Bitter memories, or another attack of fever? If she wasn't back in five minutes he'd get the waitress to go in after her. Or go in himself.

He didn't have to wait that long, just long enough to call the waiter over and arrange to pay half of the bill.

'I don't want my guest to know about it,' he said.

The waiter nodded, and left, casting a curious glance at Hannah as she came back.

Leaning back in his chair, Kelt watched her walk towards him, and something tightened in his gut. Unconsciously seductive, the exotic contours of her face were enhanced by the smile that curved her lips. Her hair gleamed in the sunlight like burnished silk, its dense darkness shot with elusive sparks of red. And the graceful sway of her hips had caught the eye of every man on the terrace.

Kelt got to his feet on a fierce rush of adrenalin, an arrogant male need to proclaim to the world that she was with him. Without thinking, he took her hand.

'All right?' he asked abruptly.

She gave him a veiled look. 'I'm fine, thank you,' she said in a tone that had an edge to it.

But her fingers trembled in his, and he could see the pulse beating in the vulnerable hollow of her throat. Fear?

No. Her colour came and went, and her eyes clung to his. A dangerous triumph burning through him, Kelt released her as the waiter came towards them.

Something had happened, Hani realised as they sat down again. Her nerves were jumping in delicious anticipation because she both wanted and feared that *something*.

But she wanted it much more than she feared it. Fortunately she had to deal with the waiter, who was trying to persuade her to order what he described as a sinfully decadent chocolate mousse.

'I'm already full, but you have some,' she urged Kelt, refusing to think of the cost.

He said, 'Not for me, but if you're having coffee I'll have some of that too.'

Still sizzling with a kind of delicious inner buzz, she surrendered to the urge to say yes, to prolong the moment. 'Coffee sounds great.'

After it had been ordered Kelt leaned back in his chair and surveyed her lazily. 'What do you plan to do while you recuperate?'

'I might write a book.'

One black brow hitched upwards. 'Do you write?'

'Not yet,' she admitted, playing with the idea. 'But everyone has to start.'

'Would you make use of your experiences in Tukuulu?'

'No, it would seem like exploiting the school and the pupils.' Another thought struck her. 'Or I could learn to paint. I've always wanted to do that.'

'The local high school has night classes, and I think there's a group that offers lessons as well,' he commented, those dispassionate eyes intent on her face. 'Anything else you can think of?'

'No,' she said quietly, some of her lovely anticipation draining away at the thought of the three long months ahead.

'You could study something that would help you with your career. There's a tertiary institute in Kaitake. Are you a New Zealand citizen?'

Through his lashes he watched her keenly, not surprised when the drawbridge came up again.

'No,' she said crisply. 'And I don't have residency either, which makes study difficult.' And prohibitively expensive.

He frowned. 'So where did you gain your qualifications?'

After a moment's hesitation she said, 'From an Auckland tertiary institute. The principal organised everything.' And the charity had paid the fees.

Uneasily she wondered whether the governing body would want repayment if she couldn't go back to Tukuulu. Brusquely she dismissed the thought; already she felt so much better. The fever had to be on the run.

Kelt said, 'If you want to study, I'd contact the same institute again. But you should make sure you're up to whatever you feel like doing.'

Years of forced independence had made such concern unusual.

And perilously sweet.

Picking up the spoon that came with the coffee, she played with it for a moment before saying with a bite to her tone, 'I certainly don't think I'm likely to collapse in public again. Apart from anything else, it might give people the wrong impression.'

His brows lifted at the allusion. 'I've apologised for my misconception,' he said with formidable detachment.

He had, so why had she reminded him of it again? Because she was reverting back to the terrified woman who'd avoided any sort of emotional connection for the past six years.

She drew in her breath to apologise in her turn, but he forestalled her by holding out his hand.

'Shake on it, and we'll forget it happened,' he said, knowing he wouldn't be able to.

From beneath lowered lids he watched her, noting the subtle signs of unease, the momentary hesitation before she held out her hand.

Why the hell was he trying to help her? If his suspicions were correct she was damaged in some way that needed professional help, possibly several years of therapy. Normally he'd stay well out of it—after making sure she got that help.

So what was different?

Hannah was different, he realised with a shock of anger and

frustration. And so was he. He was already deeper in this than he wanted to be, which meant it was time to bail out.

And even as the words scrolled through his mind, he knew he wasn't going to. This, for example—her initial involuntary flinch at his touch had eased to a certain tension.

He'd like her to welcome the feel of his hands on her skin, not be afraid of it. As she extended her hand he forced himself to be gentle, letting her control the quick handshake.

She gave him a fleeting apologetic smile when she picked up the teaspoon again, glancing away so that she accidentally met the eyes of a woman a few tables away. Skilfully made-up, with superbly cut blonde hair, clothes that made the most of some very sleek physical assets, a very opulent diamond on one elegantly manicured finger—she gave Hani a long, openly speculative stare.

Hani blinked, gave a stiff little nod and turned back to Kelt. He had noticed, of course.

'She's the soon-to-be ex-wife of one of the more notorious property developers. He's just dumped her for a woman ten years younger,' he said dismissively. 'He bought a farm further north—on the coast—and built a large and elaborate holiday house and is trying to deny the locals access to his beaches.'

As though his words had summoned her, the woman at the other table got to her feet and came across.

'Hello, Kelt.' Her smile was as fulsome as her tone, and her eyes flicked from Kelt to Hani, and back again, devouring him with a bold, open appreciation that set Hani's teeth on edge.

'Tess,' he said formally, getting to his feet.

Hani realised they were under intense covert scrutiny from the people at the other table, and wondered what was going on.

Kelt introduced Hani without giving any more information than her supposed name, and their conversation was short and apparently friendly enough, but Hani suspected that not only did Kelt disapprove of the woman, but he also disliked her.

Not that you could tell from his attitude, she thought, wondering whether she was being foolish and presumptuous. After all, she didn't *know* Kelt.

Tension knotted beneath her ribs as Tess Whoever left after one more fawning smile, and walked back to her table.

'She seems pleasant enough,' she said foolishly to fill in the charged silence when Kelt sat down again.

'I suspect I've just been put on a list of possible replacements.' He glanced at her empty coffee cup. 'Are you ready to go?'

'Yes.'

Hani half expected him to insist on paying but he made no attempt to, and to her intense relief the bill was about the amount she'd have expected to pay in a good café.

They had almost reached the turn-off to Kiwinui when she braked and drew into the side of the road.

Kelt asked, 'Something wrong?'

'I just want to look at the view,' she told him.

He nodded and got out with her, standing beside her as they looked out over a wide valley with an immense, slab-sided rocky outcrop almost in the middle.

'That's the remnant of an ancient volcanic plug,' Kelt told her. 'There are burial caves there, and—' He stopped abruptly, turning to frown at a clump of straggly trees on the side of the hill.

'What is it?' Hani asked anxiously.

Over his shoulder he said, 'I heard a noise. Listen!'

Obediently she strained to hear, but heard nothing except the soft sound of the wind in the trees. In a voice pitched barely above a whisper, she asked, 'What sort of noise?'

'A whimper, like something in pain.'

He strode towards the trees, but when Hani caught him up he stopped her with a hand on her arm, and ordered, 'Stay here.'

'Why?' The hair lifted on the back of her neck. Acutely conscious of the latent strength in the fingers curled above her elbow, she looked up into a face set in rigid lines of command.

Blue eyes hard and intent, he said, 'I don't know what it is,' he said. 'I'll go and check it out. I want you to stay here until I call you.'

'Surely you don't think—'

'I don't *know*,' he emphasised. 'And if I yell, run back to the car, lock yourself in and call emergency on the cell-phone you'll find in the glove pocket.'

When she didn't answer he said, 'Perhaps you should do that now.'

'I'll wait by the car,' she said flatly. 'But I think you're overreacting.'

He gave her a thin smile. 'Of course I am. Humour me,' he said, and watched as she walked across to stand by the vehicle.

'Be careful!' she mouthed silently as he walked into the head-high scrub.

Tensely she waited, every nerve on edge, relaxing a few minutes later when he emerged carrying a small black and white animal.

'What is it?' she asked as she ran across to him. 'Oh, it's a puppy!'

Under his breath he said something she was rather glad she couldn't hear, adding distinctly, 'And it's terrified.'

So distressed she had to swallow to control her voice, she said, 'Give it to me!' and held out her hands.

Kelt shook his head and carefully, gently manipulated each fragile limb. The puppy settled down immediately, lifting its sharp little face to him and neither flinching nor whimpering when he ran his lean, competent fingers over it.

'Get into the car and I'll drive us to the vet,' Kelt said austerely. 'It doesn't seem to be in any pain but it needs to be checked in case it's sick, or too young to be separated from its mother. In which case it will have to be put down.'

Hani quelled her instinctive outcry. She knew enough about dogs to realise that he was right.

He looked down at her and the grimness faded. 'I suppose you want to carry it?'

'Of course.'

Kelt put the squirming pup into her eager hands.

'There, there, you're all right,' she murmured, her voice low as she cuddled the little animal to her breast. Immediately it relaxed, staring earnestly up into her face.

Cradling the pup, Hani climbed into the passenger seat. 'She doesn't look sick at all,' she said when Kelt came in beside her.

'She?'

'Yes, she's a female, and she looks really healthy—fat and glossy. Her eyes are clear and bright, and she's alert. She can't have been thrown out of a car. Perhaps whoever did this wanted her to be found.'

Kelt switched on the engine and said harshly, 'If they had they wouldn't have tied her up in a sack and hidden her behind a patch of manuka scrub.'

Wishing he hadn't pointed out that inconvenient fact, she remained silent.

He must have guessed, because he sent her a swift, sideways glance. 'It's always better to face the truth,' he said. Once they were on the road he gave a humourless smile. 'Did I sound sententious and smug?'

'Yes, you did,' she told him spiritedly, stroking the puppy's downy little head. 'Unfortunately that doesn't make what you said any less true.'

'In my experience almost as much havoc is wrought by people who stubbornly make excuses for inexcusable behaviour as by the people who indulge in that behaviour.'

'Oh, dear, as well as sententious and smug you sound very old and jaded,' she teased.

To her surprise his mouth twitched at the corners, but he didn't answer, and her gaze drifted to his hands on the wheel—sure, competent, controlled...

He'd handled the pup so carefully, his long fingers gentle as he'd manipulated the tiny limbs. Into her head there sneaked an image of those hands on her skin, their lean, tanned strength a potent contrast to her pale gold.

That secret warmth blazed into life, sending a wave of hot excitement through her. Stunned, she banished the seductive fantasy and sat upright, concentrating on the animal now asleep in her lap.

But before long she stole a glance at the man beside her, unconsciously measuring the arrogant profile—all angles and straight lines except for the sexy curve of his lips.

'OK?' he asked without looking at her.

How did he know she'd been watching him? Confused by her reaction, she swallowed and said, 'Yes, she's asleep, poor little scrap. How *could* anyone be so cruel as to abandon her like that to a lingering and painful death? It's—just horrible.'

'They probably couldn't bring themselves to kill her, so they stuffed her into the sack like rubbish and dumped her— out of sight, out of mind.' Kelt's tone was coldly disgusted.

Chilled, because Felipe always had someone else do his dirty work for him, she said thinly, 'That's appalling—horrifying.'

'Indeed.'

The vet, a middle-aged woman with an expression that told them she'd seen worse things than this, said, 'She's in excellent condition. I'd say she was the only pup in the litter and that she's just been taken from her mother. She's about two months old—part border collie with something like a corgi.' She looked at Kelt, her eyes amused. 'She'll probably make a good cattle dog, Kelt.'

He smiled at that, looking at the puppy protectively cradled in Hani's arms.

'What do you want done with her?' the vet asked.

Hani said, 'I'll look after her.'

She felt the impact of Kelt's frown without seeing it, but his tone was neutral and dispassionate when he said, 'Are you sure? Puppies are a bit like babies—they need fairly constant attention and that often means getting up at night to take them outside.'

'I know.'

'You'll be sorry when you have to leave her behind.'

'Surely someone—perhaps on the station—will adopt her once I've got her housetrained and taught her some simple commands?'

'Every child on Kiwinui will want her,' Kelt said dryly, then shrugged. 'Your decision,' he said, and turned to the vet. 'Thanks for looking at her. We'd better buy some necessities before we go.'

The vet said, 'Well, let me sponsor her for that, anyway. Quite frankly, I'm glad you're not leaving me with the problem of what to do with her.'

Kelt said ironically, 'I'll stand godfather and buy her first lot of food.'

'It's all right—' When he lifted that quizzical brow Hani

stopped, realising she couldn't accept the vet's professional services then refuse Kelt's offer.

Lamely she said, 'Thank you very much, both of you.'

Halfway home Kelt asked, 'What will you call her?'

'I don't know.' She laughed. 'My brother always said dogs choose their own names if you just give them a bit of time.'

And stopped, her heart banging uncomfortably in her chest. For years she'd never spoken of Rafiq—tried not to even think of him because it hurt so much—yet somehow this man had got through her guard enough for her to mention her brother twice in as many days. She'd have to be much more careful.

He said casually, 'Your brother is probably right. You could call her Annie.'

For a horrified second she thought he'd said Hani. The puppy squirmed in her lap as though sensing the panic that kicked beneath her ribs. Then she realised what he'd actually said. Relief cracked her voice when she replied, 'Annie?'

'Little Orphan Annie, alone and friendless in the world.'

The allusion clicked into place. She kept her eyes fixed on the pup, asleep again. 'Well, she's probably not an orphan, and she's certainly not alone or friendless now—thanks to you.'

She sensed rather than saw his broad shoulders lift. 'You're the one who made the decision. I just hope you're not too shattered when you have to leave her behind.'

Hani bit her lip, then was struck by a thought. '*If* I have to leave her behind. I might be able to take her with me. I can't see why not.'

For the first time since she'd fled Felipe she was ready to risk loving again. An emotion unfurled inside her, softly and without limit, a sense of freedom and relief.

She'd believed Felipe had killed an essential part of her—

that part willing to give trust and love—when he'd ordered the death of her puppy.

But he hadn't.

It had just gone into hiding.

So she'd allow herself to love this helpless, abandoned little thing, and she'd fight to take her back to Tukuulu. After all, she'd saved the pup's life, and saving something meant it was up to you to look after it to the best of your ability.

Feeling slightly winded, as though she'd taken a huge step into the unknown, she stroked the puppy again.

'The vet said she'll grow into a working dog,' Kelt reminded her.

'So?'

'That means she'll need constant stimulation—work to occupy her mind—or she'll become frustrated and neurotic.'

Hani digested that silently before saying, 'I'll see how things go.' She sent him a quick, defiant look. 'But whatever happens, I'll always be glad we stopped to look over the valley.'

He nodded. 'Me too.'

# CHAPTER SEVEN

THE PUPPY SETTLED DOWN well in her new basket, but in the middle of the night Hani woke with a headache and the telltale signs of a bout of fever. Glumly she gulped down her medication, then remembered her promise to Kelt; aching and reluctant, she forced herself out to the telephone, squinted at the number she'd been given, and fumbled to press the buttons.

When she finally got the combination right Kelt answered. 'I'll be right down,' he said tersely. 'Get back to bed.'

By the time he arrived she was shivering under the covers, and the low hum of his approaching vehicle was probably the most wonderful sound she'd ever heard.

Learning to rely on Kelt would be almost more dangerous than falling in love with him, but at that moment she was utterly grateful he had an overdeveloped sense of responsibility.

Although she strained to hear, she didn't realise he was in the house until he opened the bedroom door and the puppy, secure in her basket in the corner of the room, woke, made a funny squeak and scrabbled at the side of her basket.

'Go back to sleep,' he said, and of course the little thing settled down again.

He came silently across to the bed and scrutinised Hani, and in spite of her heart's warning she relaxed and closed her eyes, allowing herself to yield to the effortless authority emanating from him.

'You've taken your medication?'

He frowned, because her smile was a pale imitation of the real thing. 'Yes, sir.' The words were slurred and unsteady, and she spoke with difficulty, but she added, 'I'm glad you're here.'

Kelt took her hand, surprised at the way her fingers curled around his. 'Try to relax. I'll get you a drink. Hot or cold?'

The narrow brows pleated as though she didn't understand, and a minuscule nod was followed by another shiver that racked her slender body.

'Hot,' she whispered.

He made tea and brought it in, scooping her against his chest and holding the cup to her lips as she took tiny sips of the warm liquid. He didn't know if adding sugar would help, but on the chance it might he'd sweetened it. Although her brows drew together again, she drank most of it.

To his critical eye this attack was nowhere as severe as the first one he'd witnessed, but it was bad enough. She was on fire and in pain, and there was nothing he could do but hold her and wait for the fever to subside.

He looked down at the even features, the flushed, honey-coloured skin like silk satin. She might pretend to be English, but with her superb eyes closed a heritage of more exotic bloodlines was obvious. Those eyes were set on a slight upwards tilt, their long lashes flickering and her sensuous mouth tightening as the fever burned mercilessly through her.

The thought of her enduring this alone and uncared for roused a fierce, powerful compassion in Kelt, fuelling his helpless anger at knowing the only thing he could give her was the comfort of his arms.

Eventually the fever broke dramatically, and once again she

was drenched. Relieved, he glanced at his watch. This bout was over in half the time of the previous one.

Meanwhile, what to do about her soaked clothes? She'd hate it, but she was just going to have to deal with the fact that once again he'd got her out of the wet garments and into something dry.

At the thought his body quickened, protectiveness replaced by a rush of forbidden desire. He gritted his teeth and set her back onto the bed.

Her lashes flickered again, then lifted, forced up by sheer will.

Hani stared at the dark, stony face above her, familiar yet strangely alien. Slowly her sluggish brain processed enough information for her to recall what had happened. Although exhaustion softened her bones and loosened her muscles, she shuddered at the feel of her wet hair against her throat and the clammy embrace of her clothes.

After a couple of tries she managed to say, 'Th-thank you.'

The steely blue gaze that held her prisoner didn't change. 'Do you think you can shower by yourself?'

Shying away from the only alternative, she muttered, 'Yes.'

When she tried to pull herself up he said curtly, 'Stay where you are. I'll turn the shower on and carry you in.'

But when he came back she was sitting on the side of the bed, brows knotted and panting slightly.

'I said I'd carry you in,' he said, but his tone was resigned rather than irritated.

'I can manage,' she said, defiance plain in her tone.

To her surprise he didn't object. 'OK, give it a try.'

Hani eased her feet onto the floor and grabbed the headboard, exerting the very last of her strength to stand up. Her legs shook so much that she might as well be shivering, she thought miserably.

Kelt didn't say anything; he just picked her up as effort-lessly as though she were a child and carried her across the room. As the door closed behind them she saw the puppy's eyes on them.

'I'm glad you can smile,' he said, easing her onto the chair he'd put in the shower.

'The puppy thinks we're crazy,' she managed to say, her voice wobbling.

Eyes revealing grim amusement, he examined her through a haze of steam. 'She's almost certainly right,' he told her. 'If you think you can cope, I'll leave you to it. If you can't, I'm afraid you're just going to have to grit your teeth and bear my ministrations.'

Again—only this time she was conscious. Colour prickled up from her breasts. 'I can do it,' she said quickly.

He gave her another hard stare and nodded. 'Yell if you need help,' he said succinctly, and left her.

Gathering strength, she sat for some moments just relish-ing the clean warmth of the water on her sweat-soaked body, but when she tried to get out of her clothes that same water made her clothes clinging and uncooperative. Gritting her teeth, she was able to wriggle free of her briefs, but the top resisted her every attempt.

She was shaking with useless frustration when there was a knock on the door. 'J-just a moment,' she called desper-ately, tugging at the recalcitrant shift as it refused to come over her arms.

Humiliatingly exposed, she looked around for her towel, then grabbed the one he'd put outside and wrapped it around herself. Where, of course, it immediately got wet. Hot, furious tears welled up in her eyes and ached in her throat so she couldn't produce a word.

He said, 'Hannah?'

Her silence brought him straight inside; he took in the situation immediately and said, 'It's all right.'

She flinched away as he opened the door into the shower. Face rigid, he paused for a second to strip off his shirt, then reached in and turned off the shower.

Hani could have died with embarrassment, but to her amazed bewilderment she wasn't afraid. Efficiently and without changing expression he removed her top and, while she blushed from her waist to the top of her head, he got his shirt and cocooned her in it, hiding everything down to her thighs.

'Let that wet towel drop now,' he said.

Her hands were shaking so much she couldn't even untie the one she'd knotted around her waist. Embarrassing tears filled her eyes. In a goaded voice she said, 'I f-feel so useless…'

'Nobody is at their best after a bout of tropical fever,' he said in a cool, level voice, and undid the towel for her, letting it drop.

His hands against her were—wildly exciting. They set her skin on fire.

No, they set her whole body alight. Dumbly, she stared at him, and started to shake again—delicious, fiercely erotic tremors of sensation that filled her with a tempting strength. Hani forced herself to lift her eyes from his torso—a powerful incitement in itself, strong and lean and bronze, the muscles flexing slightly as though he stayed still only with a great effort.

She met his eyes, recklessly responding to the glitter of hunger in their blue depths.

For—how long? Measured by heartbeats, an eternity. His fingers tightened around her waist, almost easing her closer, and she held her breath, everything in her focused on the warmth of his hands on her skin, the faint, primal body scent that was his alone, emphasised by the shirt she wore.

Somehow the fever had sensitised her whole body so that it longed for his touch. More than anything in the whole world she wanted him to take that final step, wanted to let her head rest on his broad shoulder, let him…

His eyes went cold, and he set her away from him, his hands closing on her shoulders to propel her out of the shower and into the bathroom.

'You need to sleep,' he said, his voice totally lacking inflection. 'Have you got a hairdryer?'

'Yes.' Every bit of passion drained away, leaving her cold and so utterly humiliated it took all her energy to produce the word.

She wanted to insist he let her walk into the bedroom, but he gave her no choice; he simply picked her up and carried her through, depositing her on the side of the bed. In spite of her bitter embarrassment Hani thought she'd never felt so safe in all her life…

'The puppy wants to go outside,' he said, and left the room.

As she shed the bath towel and struggled into a gaily-patterned wrap he'd found, she heard him talking to the puppy. The outside door rasped open, closing again a few moments later.

From the bedroom door he asked, 'Are you OK?'

'Yes.'

He came in with a dry towel, which he used to dry off her hair. He was so gentle, she thought dreamily, by now so tired she couldn't produce a coherent thought. Tomorrow she'd wake and remember what he looked like—strong and lithe, the light burnishing his tanned, powerful shoulders.

Then he turned on the hairdryer, saying grimly, 'I should have called Rosie for this part.'

Hani gave a prodigious yawn. 'You're—it's fine,' she murmured. Her half-closed gaze lingered on the scroll of dark hair across his chest.

His detachment should have reassured her. Shamefully, she was undermined by another, more searing emotion—a fierce resentment that he could be so unaffected when she felt like melting like a puddle at his feet.

Eventually he said, 'It's dry now.'

She fell onto the sheets, eyes closing as she felt the covers being pulled over her. Dimly she realised that he'd changed the bedlinen, and then exhaustion devoured her.

Kelt looked down at her. Hannah—Honey suited her much better, he thought sardonically—lay on her side, a cheek cupped in one hand, her breath coming evenly between her lips and her colour normal.

He glanced at his watch again. If she followed the previous pattern she'd sleep like that until morning, and wake up in remarkably good shape.

So he could go home to his very comfortable bed in his own room.

He picked up his shirt and pulled it on again, stopping as the faintest fragrance whispered up to him from the cloth. Jaw set, he went into the living room and opened a door onto the deck. Little waves flirted onto the sand. The tide was going out, he noticed automatically, and looked along the beach.

Mind made up, he came back in and lowered himself onto the sofa.

Hani woke to a plaintive little snuffle from the puppy, and cautiously stretched. She felt—*good*, she decided, and eased herself out of the bed.

'Yes, all right,' she said softly. 'Just give me time to find my feet…'

The medication had worked its magic; she was still a bit

wobbly, but that would go once she got some food and a cup of good coffee inside her.

Heat swept up from her throat at all-too-vivid memories of Kelt's impersonal, almost indifferent ministering to her—until the moment when his hands had released the towel around her waist.

And then, in spite of his cool self-possession, for taut, charged moments he hadn't been able to hide his desire.

For her...

Hani's breath came swiftly through her lips as she relived her own emotions—a hungry passion backed by intense confidence, as though this mutual desire was *right*, the one thing that could bring some peace and harmony to her.

OK, so he'd controlled his own reaction immediately. She wished he hadn't.

More colour flooded her skin when she remembered her dreams—tangled, happy, erotic fantasies without the shame and fear that usually dogged her night visions. Last night they'd been a fairy tale of love and passion and peace, and she'd woken with a smile.

As she scooped up the puppy and carried its wriggling body across to the door, she reminded herself that dreams were all she dared to savour as long as Felipe Gastano was alive.

She pushed the door open and stopped abruptly, eyes fixed on the man asleep on the sofa.

He'd stayed? Warmth suffused her, and a kind of wonder that he should feel so responsible for someone he didn't really know. He looked raffish, the arrogance of those strong features neither blurred nor gentled by the dark stubble of his beard.

The puppy wriggled, and she looked down at the little creature, realising that she had on only the thin cotton wrap. Torn, she half turned to get her dressing gown, but it appeared that things were getting desperate for the puppy, so she tiptoed across the room, holding her breath as she eased the door onto the lawn open.

Once placed on the grass the puppy obliged, and Hani smiled, remembering other occasions like this. Although the *castello* had been run efficiently by a team of servants, her parents had always insisted she look after her own pets.

Now, damp grass prickling the soles of her feet, she shielded her eyes against the sheen the rising sun cast on the sea, and the edge of shimmering gold outlining the big island that sheltered this coastline. Her lungs expanded, taking in great breaths of salt-scented air. She had never been in a place so beautiful, so free.

She could live here very happily, she thought wistfully. Perhaps she was attuned to living on an island in the middle of a vast sea...

Moraze was smaller than New Zealand, Tukuulu even smaller, a mere dot in the ocean, but all were thousands of miles from the nearest country, and perhaps such places bred a different kind of people.

Whatever, she could learn to love New Zealand. This part of it anyway.

The puppy sniffed its way back to her and licked her bare toes. 'Hello, little thing,' she said softly, and stooped to pick it up. 'I hope you find your name soon, because I can't go on calling you puppy, or little thing. It's demeaning. What do you think, hmm?'

The puppy swiped her chin with a pink tongue, then yawned, showing sharp white teeth in excellent condition.

On a quiet laugh Hani turned and walked back to the bach, hoping fervently that Kelt was still asleep. It seemed stupid and missish that after last night she should be so embarrassed—

the wrap covered her from neck to ankle—but she couldn't help it.

Any more than she could help that *frisson* of excitement that ran down her spine whenever she met his eyes, or the suspicious heat that smouldered into life at his lightest, least erotic touch.

Again she held her breath, keeping a wary eye on the sprawled figure dwarfing the sofa. Her breath came noiselessly between her lips as she passed the sofa, only to have that relief vanish when his rough, early-morning voice stopped her in her tracks.

'How are you feeling?'

'Good,' she blurted, turning to face him with the puppy clutched to her breast like a squirming shield. Guiltily she loosened her hold and added brightly, 'It was very kind of you to come down.'

He lifted his brows, and ran a hand across the stubble. 'There's no need to thank me.' His tone changed from the gravelly drawl to a clipped note that barely concealed anger. 'Have you had to suffer all your other attacks by yourself?'

'I managed,' she said defensively.

'Why wasn't someone with you? Once you start to shiver you have no idea what you're doing.'

Heat burned along her cheekbones. What *had* she done? Only shown him that she wanted him.

Defensively she said, 'I'm getting much better.'

'And you'd rather suffer in silence than ask for help,' he said curtly. 'But your colleagues must have known you needed help, even if you refused to ask for it.'

'I asked for it last night,' she pointed out, chin lifting.

He showed his teeth. 'You didn't, you simply told me you were coming down with another bout, and you only did that because I extracted a very reluctant promise from you.'

Her silence must have told him that he was dead on the mark. The puppy wriggled in Hani's hands again and his frown disappeared. 'Put her down. She probably wants to explore the place.'

Sure enough the little thing started to sniff the sofa leg. Hani said, 'She should know it well enough by now—she spent most of yesterday afternoon either sleeping or smelling around.'

'It will take her more than a few turns around the room to get used to being here.'

A single lithe movement brought him to his feet. Automatically Hani took a step backwards. He was so tall he loomed over her, and he had a rare ability to reduce her to a state of shaming breathlessness.

His eyes hardened. 'Why are you afraid of me?' he asked in a level voice that was more intimidating than a shout would have been.

Not that she could imagine him shouting. He'd lose his temper coldly, she thought with an inward shiver, in an icy rage that would freeze anyone to immobility.

'I'm not.' It sounded like something a schoolchild might blurt.

His brows climbed. 'If you're not afraid of me, why did you jump backwards just then, as though you think I might pounce on you?' His steel-blue eyes surveyed her mercilessly.

Very quietly, she said, 'You take up a lot of room.'

He frowned. 'What does that mean? Yes, I'm a big man, but that doesn't make me violent.'

'I know that.' She was making a total hash of this, and she owed it to him to explain that he was reaping the heritage of another man who hadn't been violent either—not in action. Felipe had never hit her. His speciality had been mental torture, a feline, dangerous malice that had irreparably scarred her.

But the words wouldn't come. After a deep breath, she continued, 'I suppose the... I feel embarrassed by being such a weakling.'

'You're not weak,' he said impatiently, 'you're ill. There's a difference.'

Rattled, she floundered for a few seconds. 'I mean, I'm grateful—'

He cut in, 'I've done no more for you or with you than your brother or father would have done. There's no need for gratitude, and certainly no need for the kind of fear you seem to feel.'

'I know,' she said quickly. 'You've been amazingly kind to me, and you don't...I don't...' She took another jagged breath. 'Look, can we just leave it?'

He said abruptly, 'Sit down.'

And when she continued to hover, he continued, 'It seems to me that you're either a virgin—'

Her abrupt headshake stopped him. The thought of Hani helpless and brutalised fanned a deadly anger inside him that demanded action. Unfortunately he had no way of finding out what had happened without forcing her to relive the experience.

Keeping his voice level and uninflected, he went on, 'Or you've had a bad experience.'

At her involuntary flinch, he said in a silky voice that sent shudders down her spine, 'So that's it.'

Hani bit her lip. 'No, actually, it's not what you're thinking.'

'Care to talk about it?'

The thought made her stomach lurch sickeningly. 'No.'

After several charged moments he said in a level, objective tone, 'You need help—therapy, probably.'

'I'm fine,' she returned, automatically defensive.

'That's your attitude to everything—just leave me alone, I'm fine,' he observed with a sardonic inflection. 'Unfortunately it doesn't seem to be working.'

Pride lifted her head. 'Sorry, I don't feel like being pyschoanalysed.' His narrowing eyes made her add tautly, 'Neither your kindness nor my gratitude gives you any right to interfere with my life.'

'The fact that you're staying in my house on my property means I've accepted some responsibility for your well-being.'

'I'm a grown woman. I'm responsible for myself—and apart from these bouts of fever I'm perfectly capable of looking after myself.'

He looked at her with an irony that was reflected in his words. 'Really? You could have fooled me.'

'That is ridiculous,' she retorted hotly. 'In fact, this whole conversation is ridiculous!'

'It's a conversation that should have taken place years ago between you and a therapist,' he said evenly. 'Before you decided that the only way to expiate the sin of being brutalised was to devote your life to doing good works.'

She went white. 'You don't know what you're talking about.'

'You flinch whenever a man comes near you. Nothing and no one has the right to do that to you.'

'I do not!'

Eyes half-concealed by those dark lashes, he covered the two paces that separated them and took her by the upper arms, holding her with a gentleness that didn't fool her—if she struggled those hands would pin her effortlessly.

Fierce heat beat up through Hani, an arousal that softened her bones and rocketed her heartbeat into panicky, eager anticipation that undermined her anger and outrage.

'You're not shaking—yet,' he said calmly. 'But if I kissed

you you'd faint. You're clenching your teeth now to stop them chattering.'

'You're an arrogant lout,' she flung at him. Desperate to banish from her treacherous mind the image of his mouth on hers, she surged on, 'Why are you doing this?'

'By *this*, do you mean holding you close?' His eyes gleamed with the burnished steel of a sword blade, but his voice was level and uninflected. 'See, you can't relax, even though you must know I won't force myself on an unwilling—or unconscious—woman.'

Neither had Felipe. He'd been able to make her want him—until she'd understood the true depths of his character, and fear and loathing had overwhelmed that first innocent, ardent attraction. And by then it was too late to run...

Still in that same neutral tone Kelt said, 'If you're afraid, Hannah, all you have to do is pull away.' He loosened his already relaxed grip.

Something—a wild spark of defiance—kept her still. A basic female instinct, honed by her past experiences, told her she had nothing to fear from Kelt—he didn't possess Felipe's cruelty, nor the lust for power that had ruled him.

And Kelt's taunt about devoting her life to good works stung. Running away had eased her visceral, primal terror for her own safety, but she'd chosen to teach because she'd wanted to help.

Staring up into the hard, handsome face of the man who held her, she realised that Kelt had somehow changed her—forcing her to face that what she was really hiding from was her own shame, her knowledge that she had let her brother down so badly.

It was as though a switch clicked on in her brain, bringing light into something she'd never dared examine. Before she could change her mind she said quietly, 'I'm not afraid of you.'

Kelt's expression altered fractionally; the glittering steel-blue of his gaze raked her face.

Hani held her breath when his mouth curved in a tight, humourless smile. 'Good.'

And she closed her eyes as he bent his head.

# CHAPTER EIGHT

HANI had no idea what to expect; eyes clamped shut, she waited, her heart thudding so noisily she couldn't hear anything else.

'Open your eyes,' Kelt ordered softly, his voice deep and sure and almost amused.

'Why?' she muttered.

His laughter was warm against her skin, erotically charging her already overwhelmed senses, but a thread of iron in his next words made her stiffen.

'So you know exactly who you're kissing,' he said.

'I do know,' she whispered. 'The man who looked after me last night.'

Impatiently, every nerve strained and eager, she waited for the touch of his lips. When nothing happened she opened her eyes a fraction and peered at him through her lashes.

In spite of the smile that curved his mouth his face was oddly stern. 'The man who wants you,' he corrected.

Colour burned her cheeks. When she realised he was waiting for an answer she mumbled, 'It's mutual.'

He gave her another intent look, one that heated until her knees wobbled. And then he bent his head the last few inches and at last she felt his mouth on hers, gentle and without passion as though he was testing her.

Into that fleeting, almost butterfly kiss she said fiercely, 'I'm *not* scared of you.'

'You can't imagine how very glad I am to hear that,' he said, his voice deep and very sure, and he gathered her closer to his lean, hardening body and kissed her again.

Hani felt something she'd never experienced before—a sensation of being overtaken by destiny, of finding her heart's one true fate.

The warnings buzzing through her brain disappeared in a flood of arousal. Kelt tasted of sinful pleasure, of erotic excitement, of smouldering sexuality focused completely on her and the kiss they were exchanging, a kiss she'd never forget.

She was surrounded by his strength and she wasn't afraid, didn't feel like a stupid child who'd fallen into a situation she didn't understand and couldn't control...

It shocked her when he lifted his head a fraction and said something. 'Hannah?'

*No, my name's Hani!* But of course she couldn't say that. Hani de Courteville no longer existed; she'd drowned six years ago. This kiss was for Hannah Court, not the pampered darling of an island nation who'd failed everyone so badly.

Opening dazed eyes, she tried to regain command of her thoughts. 'Yes?' she asked in a die-away voice.

'All right?'

From somewhere inside her she found the courage to say with a smoky little smile, 'Right now I don't think I've ever felt better. Kiss me again.'

He laughed, and she raised a hand and traced his mouth, the beautifully outlined upper lip, the sensuous lower one that supported it. Something hot and feverish coiled through her. Felipe had never wanted her caresses—forget about Felipe, she commanded wildly. He'd never made her feel like this, either—so deliciously wanton, confident in her own sexuality.

Kelt's lips closed around her finger and he bit the tip delicately, sending more erotic shivers through her.

His breath was warm against her skin when he said, 'I will, once you stop playing with my mouth.'

Greatly daring, she cupped his jaw with her two hands, relishing the opportunity as her fingertips tingled. He let her explore, and when at last she dropped her hands he caught them and pressed the palm of each to his mouth before pulling her back into his arms and kissing her again.

No butterfly touch this time, but one that frankly sought a response from her, a response she gave eagerly, losing herself in the restrained carnality of their kiss.

Until Kelt lifted his head to say on a note of laughter, 'I think your small protégé needs another run outside.'

'Oh!' She pulled away, hiding her disappointment by bending to pick up the puppy, which was making plaintive noises at her feet.

'I'll take her,' he said crisply.

She handed the puppy over and while he took it through the door into the sunlight she dashed into the bathroom and combed her tumbled hair into some sort of order.

More of those sexy little chills ran through her as she remembered him holding her head still while he'd kissed her, doing with his mouth what her fingers had done to the jut of his chin and the clean, unyielding line of his jaw.

She'd been completely lost in passion, so far gone that nothing but Kelt's kiss had been real to her. She hadn't even heard the puppy.

But Kelt had.

'Oh, dear God,' she whispered, pressing a cold cloth to her hot cheeks and tender mouth.

Was she doomed to be attracted to inherently cold men totally in control of their emotions, their passions?

After she'd realised that Felipe's interest in her had been only because she was Rafiq de Courteville's sister, she'd vowed never to lose her head over a man again.

But Kelt had been so kind, some pathetic part of her pleaded. Felipe had teased and amused her, flattered and caressed her, but she could never remember him being kind...

OK, so Kelt wasn't like Felipe, but he was still dominant, accustomed to being in charge.

So was Rafiq.

Tormented, she stared at her reflection—big dark eyes still slumberous in her flushed face, her trembling mouth full and well-kissed. She simply didn't know Kelt well enough to even guess what sort of man he really was.

Quite probably he'd kissed her on a whim—or because he'd rather liked what he'd seen when he'd helped her out of the shower.

He certainly couldn't feel anything more for her than a physical desire.

But that's what you want, she reminded herself. This is just sexual passion, nothing more. You're not in love with him. You don't want him to love you.

*Yes, I do.*

With a horrified inward groan, she turned away and grabbed a towel, hiding her face in it for a second before turning to face her reflection.

All right, she silently told the wanton woman in the mirror, falling in love with Kelt Gillan is simply not an option. So you'll call a halt right now. Yes, it's going to make you feel like an idiot, but you've been behaving like one, so it serves you right.

She dried her face, applied a light film of gloss to her mouth, then turned away, squaring her shoulders, and walked out into the sitting room just as Kelt, this time with the puppy gambolling at his heel, walked through the French door into the room.

Her gaze skipped from broad shoulders to the width of his chest and the narrow, masculine hips. One of those sensuous little shivers scudded down her backbone.

Abruptly, before she could change her mind, she blurted, 'I hope you don't think that this…ah, those…what we did…'

'Those kisses?' he supplied smoothly.

His cool, confident tone gave her the strength to say stolidly, 'Yes. I hope you don't think they meant anything.'

'Beyond that you want me?' This time his voice was cynically amused.

'Exactly,' she said, almost cringing at the undercurrent of embarrassment in the word. However, having handed him the opportunity to mock her, she just had to wear it with as much grace as she could.

Quailing inside, she called on every scrap of courage she possessed to meet his coolly measuring survey with a pretence of confidence.

'I assume you're trying to tell me that, just because you kissed me with enthusiasm and a charming lack of pretence, it doesn't mean you're going to sleep with me,' he said blandly.

Shaken by his bluntness, Hani bought a moment by stopping to pick up the puppy, who licked her chin lavishly and promptly dozed off.

'That's exactly what I mean.' She prayed she could bring this awkward and humiliating conversation to an end without seeming any more foolish than she already did.

He said with cutting emphasis, 'A few kisses, however hungry and sweet, don't constitute an invitation to sex, so you can relax. Don't ever judge me again by whatever bastard made you so afraid of men. When I feel the urge to take you to bed, I'll make sure you know well ahead of time, and I'll let you make the decision.'

Hani said in a goaded voice, 'I'm sorry—'

'Like your gratitude, an apology isn't necessary,' he cut in without emphasis. He looked down at the sleeping puppy. 'Has she decided on a name for herself yet?'

Hani forced herself to respond. 'I don't think Sniffer would be a nice name for a puppy,' she said, hoping he didn't notice her brittle tone. 'I'll wait a few days, and if she doesn't come up with something more suitable I'll have to choose a name myself.'

Kelt nodded. 'In spite of what your brother said. Where is he, by the way?'

Hating the lie, Hani said shortly, 'He's dead,' and turned away. 'I'll just put her in her basket.'

He stopped her with one hand. 'I'll go back to the homestead,' he said, blue eyes hooded and unreadable as he scanned her face. 'But just for your information—although I find you very attractive, you're quite safe with me. And if you're thinking that naturally I'd say that—'

Wishing she could deal with this with a light hand and not make blunder after blunder, she broke in, 'Look, it's not important. Truly. I suppose I overreacted—just like you did when you heard her whimpering.' Colour high, she met his opaque gaze with desperate candour. 'Of c-course I find you attractive too, but I'm not—I don't want to embark on an affair that will have to stop when I go back to Tukuulu.'

Kelt's arrogant black brows drew together. 'You must

realise by now that this latest bout of fever reduces your chances of going back to Tukuulu.'

She stared at him. 'What do you mean?'

His frown deepened. 'If you go back to the tropics the fever could well recur.'

'That's not much of a problem; the medication works every time. You've seen how well I respond to it.'

He said harshly, 'Constant use produces a raft of quite nasty side-effects.'

Her eyes widened, then went blank. 'The attacks are getting further and further apart.'

'Because you're in New Zealand,' he told her with brutal honesty. 'People can become permanent invalids from this, Hannah. Some still die. If you go back to Tukuulu that's a possibility the school has to take into account.'

Grabbing for composure, she babbled, 'No, that won't happen. The medication works really well.'

'How well are *you* going to work if you keep having attacks? How much use will you be to the school?' He switched subjects. 'As for the side-effects—do you have a computer?'

She shook her head.

'Then come up to the homestead and I'll show you the information I found in a search that took me five minutes.'

Torn, she hesitated, but this was important. 'I have to get dressed—'

Ten minutes later, clad in trousers and one of her new jerseys, she found herself inside his Range Rover, the puppy in her lap. While Kelt drove silently towards his house she stared out through the window, worrying away at his statement.

Stop it, she told herself sturdily. He might be wrong.

But he wasn't a man who made mistakes.

Though hadn't she read somewhere that only the naïve trusted everything they'd read on the internet?

It wasn't until she sat in front of his sophisticated computer set-up in his scarily modern office that panic closed in on her, producing something terrifyingly close to nausea.

'How do I know this is accurate?' she asked thinly, staring at the words that danced on the screen. She blinked several times and they settled down, spelling out a frightening message.

'Because it comes from a respected medical journal.' He waited, noticing the absolute rigidity of her spine, as though if she relaxed something might shatter. Frowning, he said, 'Finish it.'

Dark head bowed, she read silently and swiftly. Once she finished she didn't turn to look at him, but dropped her gaze to the keyboard.

And when at last she spoke her voice was flat and completely without emotion. 'I wish they'd told me.'

'Your doctor should have,' he said, coldly angry because nobody seemed to care much about her.

'He's old, and...' She couldn't go on.

'It's not the end of the world,' he said calmly. 'A couple of years in a temperate climate will almost certainly make sure you recover.' Without giving her time to digest that he went on, 'Do you want me to get in touch with the expert in tropical medicine they quote?'

She couldn't afford some expensive expert. And if she couldn't get back to Tukuulu... Panic kicked Hani beneath the ribs, temporarily robbing her of rationality.

She had nowhere else to go, nothing else she could do. Her homeland was forever banned to her. Rafiq would never forgive her for putting him through the agony of losing a sister who'd not only figured in a sleazy scandal, but had also tried to take the easy way out by committing suicide.

Besides, he was married now, and a father. She'd picked up an elderly magazine in the hospital in Tukuulu, and seen a photograph of the ruling family of Moraze—a wife who'd looked like someone Hani could love, and two handsome sons. Rafiq had other people to love, closer to him than a sister could ever be.

She'd felt she was doing something worthwhile in her job on Tukuulu, but if she couldn't go back…

Her godmother's inheritance wouldn't support her, and she suspected that her qualifications wouldn't help her find a job in New Zealand unless she actually emigrated. And she didn't want to do that; it would mean too much enquiry into her past.

Kelt said crisply, 'I'll make an appointment with the specialist.'

'No,' she said thinly. She turned and met his eyes, shivering a little at the burnished sheen that made them unreadable.

'Why not? If you're worried about money—'

'No,' she repeated more briskly this time, and got to her feet, taking in a deep breath as he put out a hand to help her.

Hani ignored it, but in spite of the scared thoughts churning in her brain, his closeness triggered a swift, uncontrollable excitement. His kisses had sensitised her to him, linking them in some intangible way so that her body ached with forbidden longing.

What was he thinking?

She tried to smile. 'If that's true, then it looks as though my time on this side of the world could soon be over,' she said, struggling to project a voice that sounded light and casual.

So much for thinking she could learn to love this place!

'You'll go back to the UK?' Kelt asked neutrally.

'Where else?' she said, trying to avoid a direct lie. She hated the falsehoods her foolish decisions forced on her; they made her feel cheap and dirty, a woman tarnished by her many mistakes.

Kelt's scrutiny hardened, and this time the shiver down her spine had little to do with the erotic physical excitement he conjured in her. Apprehension was a much colder, more threatening sensation.

'If you don't want to go back to England you could always stay here.' His tone and expression gave nothing away.

In spite of that, her foolish heart leapt in her breast. Hastily she said, 'Emigrate? I doubt very much that I have any skills New Zealand requires.'

'We always need good teachers. You'd probably have to do some more teacher training, but I'm sure you could manage that.'

She didn't dare. If anyone ever suspected that Hannah Court was the supposedly dead sister of Rafiq de Courteville, ruler of the island of Moraze, the news would be splashed across the world media, just as her death had been! In Tukuulu she'd arrived as a tourist, her passport barely glanced at. Once she'd been asked to stay on at the school she'd been accepted with no further enquiries.

Coming into New Zealand on leave had been simple enough, but emigration was a whole different affair. She struggled to control her fear, reminding herself that her passport was perfectly legitimate. Her mother had been the daughter of the ruler of a small Middle Eastern state, and her children held dual citizenship.

But emigration officials might probe deeper than that. She didn't dare take the chance.

Shrugging, she said lightly, 'Well, I'll wait until I know for certain whether I can go back to Tukuulu.' She gave the computer a quick glance. 'But thanks for finding that information for me. Just in case, I'll do some serious thinking about the future while I'm here.'

'Get better first,' he advised, still in that coolly objective tone. He indicated the puppy, snoozing on a rug. 'And find a name for that dog.'

Pretending an amusement she didn't feel, she said wryly, 'Right now, I think Sleepy would be perfect.'

A knock turned his head. 'Yes?'

Arthur peered around the door. After a quick smile at Hani he said succinctly, 'Your cousin's here.'

'Thanks,' Kelt said, his voice giving nothing away.

'I'll walk back,' Hani said immediately. Right then she didn't feel like dealing with the ebullient and rather too frank Rosie Matthews.

'Nonsense,' Kelt said, black brows meeting for a second as he looked down at her.

Rosie appeared in the doorway, looking theatrically stunned. 'Good heavens—you've let her into the inner sanctum!' she exclaimed. 'What an honour! He must be in love with you, Hannah! Nobody ever gets into Kelt's office—it's *verboten*!' She stared around as though she'd never seen it before.

Although Kelt's mouth curved, he said evenly, 'Knock it off, Rosie. All those exclamations will frighten the puppy.'

*'Puppy?'* Her mobile features softened when her gaze fell on the small animal curled up on the mat. 'Oh, what a charmer,' she crooned, and glided gracefully into the room. 'But not your style, Kelt—it looks a definite bitser. You like brilliantly pedigreed Labs.'

Briefly he explained the circumstances of the puppy's arrival.

Rosie looked at Hani with interest. 'What are you going to call her?'

'I suggested Annie,' Kelt told her.

'As in Little Orphan?' When he nodded, she said indignantly. 'No, that's horrible. Besides, she isn't an orphan any longer.'

Hani said, 'She'll find her own name soon enough.'

Rosie looked up at her cousin and fluttered her lashes. She had, Hani noticed with a hint of chagrin, very long, very curly lashes.

'Actually, Kelt,' she said in a syrupy voice that made Hani's mouth curve, 'I came to ask a favour.'

One black brow lifted. 'Ask away.'

She sighed. 'I don't know how just lifting one eyebrow is so intimidating, but it works every time,' she complained.

'Stop stalling.'

Hani said, 'Perhaps Rosie would prefer to talk to you alone.'

'She would not,' Rosie said immediately. She took a swift breath and said, 'I thought you might like to give a party.'

Kelt asked, 'Why can't your mother do it?'

'Because she's in Borneo.'

This time both brows rose. 'Your mother?' Kelt asked with an edge to his voice. 'In Borneo? I thought she was going to Auckland to the opera.'

Rosie shrugged elaborately. 'Well, this new man in her life has a thing about orang-utans, and there's this place where they introduce baby ones back into the wild. She thought she'd rather do that than see *Carmen* again, especially as she doesn't like the tenor—'

'Spare me,' Kelt cut in dryly. 'So why can't you ask your father to give you this party?'

Rosie sent him a look. 'You know very well he's writing another book.' Her tone indicated that this was answer enough.

'I'll remind him he has a daughter,' Kelt said grimly.

Kelt's open protectiveness for his cousin reminded Hani of

her brother; he too had been protective—possibly too much so. If she'd had half of Rosie's sophistication she might not have fallen for Felipe.

'No, don't do that,' Rosie said swiftly.

Kelt frowned, but didn't press the issue. 'Who do you want to invite?'

'Oh, just the usual crowd.' Rosie looked vague.

Relentlessly Kelt asked, 'Who in particular?'

Flushing, his cousin admitted, 'There's this man—he's staying with the O'Hallorans at their bach. I thought it would be a neighbourly thing to have a party for them.'

'What's his name?'

With an exasperated glower Rosie said, 'Alonso de Porto, but he's got a stack of other names to go with that. He's from Spain. He's been doing a grand tour of New Zealand.'

Hani froze, her skin leached of all colour, and beads of sweat burst out at her temples. Desperately she stooped and picked up the puppy, hoping the abrupt movement would hide her shock.

# CHAPTER NINE

YAWNING sleepily, the pup snuggled into the cup of Hani's hands. She kept her eyes on it for as long as she could, forcing her mind into action.

The Alonso de Porto she'd known was a handsome boy who'd hung about on the fringes of Felipe's circle for a few weeks until his parents whisked him out of harm's way.

It couldn't be the same man. New Zealand was as far from the jet-setting sophistication of Europe as he could get.

Or be sent.

After all, if his parents had sensibly removed him from Felipe's influence once, possibly they'd had to do it again. But to New Zealand?

Entirely too much of a coincidence, she thought frantically, all her illusions of safety shattered.

Could Felipe have found her and sent Alonso…?

She took a deep breath. Why would Felipe use a Spanish grandee to track her down when he had professionals to do that sort of thing?

But if it *was* the Alonso she remembered, would he remember her?

She tried to calm her racing heart and dispel the coldness spreading beneath her ribs. When they'd met she'd been at university, struggling to fulfil her study obligations in spite of Felipe's obstruction, so she hadn't seen a lot of young de Porto.

And then relief washed through her as she realised she'd been so busy panicking she hadn't thought of the most obvious way of avoiding discovery. All she had to do was stay safely hidden at the bach!

Forcing herself to relax, she let her lashes drift cautiously up. Her stomach clamped when she met Kelt's cool, hard scrutiny. *He knows,* she thought for a taut second, feeling the familiar chill of shame.

But of course he couldn't.

Easing her grip on the squirming puppy, she parried Kelt's gaze with all the composure she could produce, forcing her brows upwards in a questioning look.

'I think I've met him,' Kelt said neutrally. 'A nice enough kid, and surprisingly unspoiled for the scion of a Spanish family with a pedigree that goes back a thousand years or so, and a fortune to match.'

Oh, God, that sounded like the Alonso she knew…

She steadied her breath, willing her heartbeat to settle down and her legs to stop shaking.

Rosie glared at Kelt, then laughed. 'Of course, you know everyone who's anyone, don't you? Although it's a bit daunting to hear the best-looking man I've ever seen described as *"a nice enough kid"*. Kid? He can only be four or five years younger than you!'

Kelt eyed her with amusement. 'All right, you can have this party, but you'll organise it yourself. Arthur will have enough to do with the cooking.'

'Super.' Rosie hurled herself into his arms, kissed his cheek with fervour, then tore free.

Hani felt a pang of—jealousy? Surely not, she thought, horrified.

That horror was intensified by Rosie's next enthusiastic words. 'I thought a nice *casual* party, a beach-and-barbecue sort of thing, starting around seven because it's such a super time in summer. One for Hannah—to introduce her to everyone.'

'So it could,' Kelt said, his keen gaze on Hani's face.

Stricken, she said as lightly as she could, 'Oh, no, you mustn't. A summer party doesn't need a reason beyond the season, surely?'

'But this would be perfect!' Rosie swept on. 'After all, if you're going to be here for three months you might as well meet all the usual suspects. And their visitors,' she added with a brilliant smile.

'Just remember Hannah's here to convalesce,' Kelt said. He gave his cousin a direct, intimidating look. 'I don't want her roped into helping you.'

'Cross my heart,' Rosie said after a speculative glance at Hani.

'I'm getting better, not dying,' Hani said briskly, earning herself another thoughtful look from the younger woman.

'Cool. We must get together some time and have lunch,' Rosie said, then blew an airy kiss to Kelt and whirled out of the room, leaving Hani breathless.

So much for hiding…

Still, she had the perfect excuse—her illness.

To the sound of his cousin's teasing voice in the hall and Arthur's indulgent replies, Kelt said ironically, 'Don't let her bulldoze you into doing anything you don't want to.'

'That's very thoughtful of you,' Hani said, 'but I wish you hadn't given her the impression that you had any right to monitor my behaviour.'

'I doubt if she's at all surprised. She frequently tells me I'm arrogant and overbearing, not to mention inflexible and old-fashioned.'

'She knows you well,' Hani said on a false, sweet note.

Kelt's answering smile sent excitement curling through her. His kisses were thrilling, but his smile had the power to reduce her to abject surrender. Not that it softened the hard lines of his face, but there was genuine humour behind it, and an appreciation of her tart irritation with him.

'I'm the big brother she never had,' he said. 'Or possibly the father. Her own is so wrapped up in his work he can only see her as an interruption.'

Hani's face must have shown what she thought of this, because he said, 'Oh, he loves her, but more when she's at a distance. That's why she lives with her mother.'

'Poor Rosie,' she said involuntarily. 'What sort of books does her father write?'

'He's a historian.' He gave her a sardonic look as though expecting her to be bored. 'At the moment he's writing a tome on Chinese exploration in the Indian Ocean; he's planning to head off to Moraze, an island a thousand miles or so off the coast of Africa, to research some ruins there. He's convinced they're Chinese.'

Hani froze. She knew those ruins.

It seemed everything—from Alonso de Porto to Rosie's father's sphere of interest—was leading back to her old life.

Oppressed by a feeling of bleak inevitability, she said brightly, 'How interesting. And don't worry about me—I won't overdo things.' Grateful for the excuse he'd given her, she said, 'I doubt if I'll get to Rosie's party so I'll make sure she doesn't use me as the reason for it.'

'Leave Rosie to me,' he said briefly. 'You look as though you could do with a cup of tea. Or coffee, perhaps.'

Right then she just wanted to get away and hide. The unexpected links between her old life and her new had shattered her precarious composure. She produced a smile, hoping he'd put its perfunctory nature down to tiredness. 'Thank you, but actually I'd rather go back to the bach.'

And met his keen survey with as limpid and innocent a look as she could manage.

His brows drew together but he said evenly, 'Of course. Rosie tends to have that effect on people. If we could harness her energy we'd probably earn megabucks from selling it to the national grid.'

Hani's gurgle of laughter brought an answering smile to his mouth, but the hard eyes were still uncomfortably intent.

So she said brightly, 'I can walk back. I could do with some fresh air.'

'I'll take you back.'

And that was that. He left her at the bach with an injunction to rest, and a feeling of being safe and protected by his concern.

You don't need care and concern, some tough inner part of her warned.

After all, she'd been independent for six years, forging her own way. And in the process she'd discovered things about herself: that she was good with children, that she could teach, that she liked the satisfaction of working hard and making a difference. Life at Tukuulu had shown her that she could cope without the protective influence of her older brother.

Her mind skittered away from the memory of Kelt's kisses. One lesson she'd learned thoroughly before she washed up on Tukuulu was that men didn't necessarily feel anything for the women they made love to. Felipe had seen her as a tool he could use, deliberately wooing and seducing her with no more emotion than lust and a desire for power.

Oh, he'd enjoyed their lovemaking; with a shudder she thought he'd found some vile satisfaction in debauching innocence.

Driven by restlessness, she got to her feet. 'How about a walk on the beach, little one?' she said to the puppy.

Once breathing in the clean, salt-scented air, the sun warm on her head and the sand firm and cool beneath her bare feet, with the puppy snuffling happily around a piece of dried seaweed, she thought that at least there had been no undercurrent of exploitation in Kelt's kisses; he'd treated her as an adult fully aware of what she was doing. And she'd been gripped by a far more primal, intense chemistry than when she'd been so sure she was in love with Felipe.

A sweet, potent warmth washed through her. She didn't dare let things go any further, but she'd always treasure the memory of Kelt's kisses.

And not just his kisses. Somehow, just by being his masterful, enigmatic, uncompromising self, by looking after her, even because of the way he dealt with Rosie, he'd restored her faith in men.

But was it wise to trust her instincts?

'Probably not,' she said to the puppy, who startled them both with a high-pitched yap.

The little animal sat back on its haunches and stared at Hani as though suspecting that the noise had come from her.

'Hey, you can talk!' She bent to stroke her, and received a lick on the wrist and another little yap.

'OK, that clinches it,' Hani said, chuckling. 'You've found your name. How do you do, Gabby?'

Gabby cocked her head, then yapped again and scratched

herself with vigour, sending a spray of sand a few centimetres into the air.

Hani felt tears burn her eyes. It had been so long since she'd dared to love; the puppy had broken through her protective armour, opening her to emotions she'd shunned for six dark years.

Actually, no—meeting Kelt had cracked that shell she'd constructed around herself with such determination.

She stooped to pick up a bleached piece of driftwood and drew a pattern in the sand. Just because she'd met a man who made her feel like a woman with heated passions and deepseated needs didn't mean she could allow Kelt to become important to her in any way. Caution warned her that this new-found capacity to feel could hurt her all over again.

The puppy came up to investigate this new activity, pounced on the stick and promptly fell over.

'Oh, poor baby!' Hani said, then watched, intrigued, as Gabby got up and sank her tiny needle-teeth into the wood, growling fiercely.

'You've probably got it right, Gabby,' she said aloud. 'Fall over, pick yourself up and start over again. And again if necessary. Perhaps that's what I should have done instead of running away.'

Except that she'd had bigger issues to deal with than a dose of heartbreak—staying alive and out of Felipe's clutches being the most important.

Resolutely pushing the grim memories to the back of her mind, she walked up to the bach, stopping halfway to rescue the exhausted Gabby, who drank lavishly once they got back then sprawled out in the sunlight on the floor and went to sleep.

Smiling, Hani made herself a snack and sat down to eat it,

but pushed it away as the memories intruded. Could Alonso still be part of Felipe's circle?

If he was, and he recognised her and mentioned it to Felipe, she'd be in danger. Before she'd 'died' she'd told Felipe she was leaving him.

He'd been quite calm about his response, wielding his power with consummate artistry. 'Of course you may go if you no longer want to stay with me. But if you do, you will be signing your brother's death warrant as well as your own.' He'd watched the colour drain from her skin and smiled. 'And neither his death nor yours will be quick,' he'd said calmly.

Desperately she got to her feet and walked the length of the terrace, her haunted eyes ignoring the beauty before her.

That was what had pushed her into informing Rafiq that Moraze was threatened, and her despairing decision to kill herself. Although she hadn't managed to achieve that, she'd managed to convince the world she was dead, buying six years in a peaceful limbo.

If those years had taught her anything, it was that losing your head only made things worse.

First of all, she needed to know if this Alonso de Porto was the same one she'd known back then, and if he still made up part of Felipe's circle.

If only she had a computer she could go onto the internet and search for Felipe's name. He'd be easy enough to track down—presumably he still figured in the social pages of various glossy magazines.

If Alonso was still part of his circle she'd have to leave Kiwinui.

Running again, around and around like a rat in a cage...

Although she'd occasionally used the one school computer

she'd never dared look for Felipe, or even for Rafiq and Moraze. Tracking software enabled the teachers to check on the sites the students visited.

Into her mind there sprang the image of the superb set-up in Kelt's office. No doubt he needed to keep up-to-date with farming matters, but a smile hovered on her lips because it seemed the impregnable farmer was a techno-freak.

He had no children to guard, so there'd be no need for him to have tracking software.

She could ask…something…and if he offered her the use of his computer…

Appalled, she pushed the idea away.

But during the rest of the afternoon it came back to her again and again, and that night it vied with other, more tender images of Kelt's kisses, until in the end she woke sobbing from a nightmare in which Kelt had morphed into Felipe.

Shaking, she made herself a cup of tea and sat out on the deck watching the sea wash gently in and out on the beach, the moon catching the white tips of the waves as they broke into lacy patterns on the sand.

She'd been passive for too long. Now she needed to take charge of her life. And she could only do that if she had information.

And then she remembered seeing an internet café close to the pet shop.

'Oh, for heaven's sake!' she whispered.

So much for taking charge of her life! Why on earth hadn't she thought of that hours ago? No need to ask Kelt—no need to do anything more frightening than pay for half an hour of internet access. 'Tomorrow,' she promised herself, half-terrified, half-eager.

The next morning Kelt rang. 'I'm going into town

shortly,' he said, 'and I wondered if you need anything or if you'd like to come.'

Hani's first instinct was to say no, and drive into town later when he was safely home again. But she thought of passing his house, or just possibly seeing him on the farm...

So she said, 'Well, yes, as it happens I do.'

'I'll pick you up in half an hour.' He rang off.

The day was warm, so she chose a pair of loose-fitting cotton trousers the same green as her eyes, and topped them with a neat cap-sleeved T-shirt that matched her skin colour. All she needed to complete the theme, she thought with wry humour as she applied lip gloss, were black shoes that gleamed red in the sun like her hair. Failing those, she made do with a pair of tan sandals.

'I won't be too long,' she promised Gabby, who blinked at her and went straight back to sleep.

Her heart jumped when the car came down the hill, and jumped again when Kelt got out. What he did to her nerve cells, she thought with an involuntary shiver, was positively sinful...

He subjected her to a long, considering look, then smiled. 'You've obviously been sleeping very well.'

'I have,' she replied, hoping her sedate tone didn't tell him that it was his presence that gave her cheeks colour and lightened her step.

Kelt closed the door behind her and slid behind the wheel. 'And how is the puppy?'

'Her name is Gabby.' Hani grinned at his cocked eyebrow. 'She's just discovered that she can yap, and she's been practising often. But she only woke me once last night.'

All morning she'd been fighting a faint nausea at the prospect of seeing even a photograph of Felipe again, but Kelt's arrival had put paid to that. In his company everything seemed at once infinitely more complex, yet straightforward; colours were brighter, scents more seductive. His presence sharpened her appreciation of the blue of the sky and the brilliant green of the fields—*paddocks*, she corrected herself with a half-smile—and the stark loveliness of the countryside.

It wasn't exactly comfort—let alone comfortable—but she was buoyed by a sense of exhilaration, a feeling that life could be filled with richness and delight if she allowed herself to deserve it.

That newly awakened confidence faded fast once she walked into the internet café. Heart pounding and the nausea returning in full force, she sat down and keyed in the search engine, then glanced around. There were only two other people there—tourists—and they couldn't have been less interested in her.

Twenty minutes later she paid her money and sat down limply at one of the tables, waiting for the strong black coffee she'd ordered.

Felipe was dead. The words echoed in her head. He'd died on Moraze four years ago in a shoot-out with the military. The news items had been brief and carried very little information. Clearly Rafiq had clamped a lid on Press speculation.

Hani waited for relief, for joy, for anything but this vast emptiness. Nothing came.

She could go back home.

No, she could never go back. Rafiq wouldn't welcome her—how could he, when she'd caused him so much grief and pain?

She had chosen to die, and it would be far better for those she'd left behind if she stayed as dead as they thought her. She glanced around the shop, the customers drinking tea and coffee, the people walking the streets outside, the sights and smells of normality…

Here she could build a new life. The thought lingered. No one knew her here. She could start afresh...

Her mind returned to those moments she'd spent in Kelt's arms, his mouth on hers producing such ecstatic excitement that she could feel it now in every cell of her body, like a delicious electric current that revived joy and brought a kind of feverish hope.

'Hannah?'

Kelt's hard voice broke in on her scattered thoughts, making her jump. Thank God, she thought in a spill of relief, she'd finished at the computer before he came in.

The concern in his tone warmed her. 'Oh—hi. I'm waiting for my coffee.' Surprisingly, her voice was level. She indicated the chair opposite her. 'Why don't you join me?'

The coffee arrived then, and he ordered for himself, then settled back in his chair and said, 'You looked—a bit disconnected.'

She shrugged. 'Just daydreaming.'

'About what?'

'Nothing,' she said instantly, flushing under his sardonic gaze.

His beautiful mouth tightened. 'It didn't seem a pleasant daydream.'

'Daydreams are pleasant by definition, surely?' She drank some of her coffee. The excitement he roused in her returned, bringing with it the feeling that everything could work out, that the world was a better place when she was in Kelt's company. She set the cup down on its saucer and finished, 'Anything else would be a daymare, and I don't think there is such a thing.'

## CHAPTER TEN

HANI said lightly, 'The thing about daydreams is that we control them, so they're always wish-fulfilment. Therefore they're always pleasant.'

Kelt eased his big body back into the chair. 'So tell me, what's your favourite daydream?'

She stared at him, saw his mouth curve, and said demurely, 'When I was five it was to be a bareback rider in a circus. I wanted to wear a short, frilly skirt with sequins all over it, and have long, golden hair that floated behind me while I rode a huge white stallion around the ring. What was yours?'

'When I was five?'

He accepted the coffee from the waitress, a woman who'd given Hani only a perfunctory smile. Her interest in Kelt was obvious, her smile broader and tinged with awareness, her eyes lingering on his hard, handsome face.

Hani squelched the same unwelcome prickle of jealousy she'd felt when Rosie had kissed him. Darn it, she thought in frustration, she was behaving like an idiot, so caught up in his male physical magic that she'd lost all sense of proportion.

OK, so he'd kissed her, and she'd kissed him back, lost in some rapturous wonderland she'd never experienced before. But honing a natural talent to his present expertise probably meant he'd kissed a lot of women. It was just plain stupid to feel that his care for her when she'd been feverish had somehow impressed her body so much it craved his touch.

'When you were five,' she reminded him once the waitress had reluctantly taken herself off.

Broad shoulders lifted in a slight shrug. 'A very boring ambition, nothing as romantic as yours; I wanted to be an astronaut, the first man to stand on Mars. Then I decided that an explorer—Indiana Jones-style—would be even more interesting. We had an old bullocky—a bullock driver—living on Kiwinui then, and he showed me how to use a whip. The first time I got it to crack I thought I'd reached the pinnacle of life's achievements.'

When she laughed delightedly, he smiled. 'That was just before my pirate period, when I roared around the Caribbean on my ship with a loyal crew of desperadoes and gathered vast amounts of treasure.'

Hani had a sudden glimpse of him as he must have been—always a leader, even as a child, his innate authority bred in him.

She opened her mouth to tell him that Moraze had an interesting history of fighting against and sometimes in alliance with the corsairs who'd once infested the Indian Ocean. Just in time, she called back the words, but he'd noticed.

He always noticed, she thought, confused by mixed emotions.

'You were going to say?' he prompted.

She summoned a smile. 'Just that we've both proved my point—it's impossible to have unpleasant daydreams because we always star in them.'

'You have an interesting habit of appearing to be about to speak, only to check yourself and come out with a platitude.'

His voice was conversational, but when she glanced up at him his eyes were uncomfortably keen.

She parried, 'Learnt from experience; teachers who blurt out comments or statements without thinking first can get themselves into trouble.'

Although he gave her abraded nerves a chance to settle down by steering the conversation into neutral channels, she suspected that every slip of her tongue was filed away in his mind.

But on the way home he asked, 'What are your plans if you aren't able to return to Tukuulu?'

Tension tightened her skin. 'I'll leave making plans for when I'm sure I can't go back—*if* that happens.'

'So you're determined to return if you can?' At her nod he said with cool detachment, 'You're a very dedicated teacher.'

'It's what I do.'

Again she endured that penetrating survey. 'No daydreams of children of your own, a husband, of falling in love?'

Her chin came up. 'I could ask you the same question,' she evaded. 'After all, you're quite a bit older than I am.'

'I'm thirty.'

'Well, why—at six years older than I am—are you still single?'

He looked amused. 'I haven't met anyone I'd like to marry.'

'Same with me.' And that, she thought with a quiver of pain, was yet another lie to add to her list.

He undercut her momentary triumph by saying, 'So we're both unattached.'

His tone hadn't altered but something—an edge to his words that hadn't been there before—set her senses onto full alert. 'I am,' she said, holding on to her reserve with determination.

'I am also. Completely.'

Hani had no idea how to reply to this, or what to do. Was

this how he wooed a possible lover, or was he warning her off? Excitement roiled through her in a series of sparks, setting fire to her imagination and her body.

Why not? Why not follow this wildfire attraction and see where it led?

Kelt wasn't like Felipe. She knew that in her innermost heart.

No, it was impossible. She realised they were passing the stream where she'd seen him digging out the blockage. Felipe would have considered such work degrading.

Just *stop* this, she told herself. Stop comparing Kelt to Felipe.

She said, 'So none of the women Rosie has comforted meant anything to you?'

His expression was amused. 'Rosie is a born exaggerator,' he said dryly, 'and you realised that five minutes after meeting her, so don't use her to back up your decision.'

A decision? As the car approached the bach, she gathered the courage to say carefully, 'I'm not sure what's going on here.'

He didn't reply until he'd stopped the car and switched off the engine. His silence was too intimidating, she thought, and scrambled out, turning to face him with her chin held high as he came around the car to stand in front of her.

His expression unreadable, he asked, 'How old were you when you went to Tukuulu?'

After a moment's hesitation she answered, 'Eighteen.'

'Barely more than a child,' he said, frowning. 'What the hell were your family thinking?'

'I have no family,' she said, hating the lie.

'And since then you've had no relationships?'

'That's none of your business,' she said coldly, aware that heat was emphasising her cheekbones.

'In other words you haven't.'

Reduced to frustrated silence by his blunt statement, she gave him a haughty glare and started off down the path towards the bach.

From behind he said deliberately, 'I'm trying to tell you that I find you very interesting—and very desirable. Did you enjoy being kissed?'

Keeping her head down, she groped in her bag for the key and said the first thing that came into her head. 'If I hadn't I'd have slapped your face.'

Oh, how banal! Hastily, her skin by now scorching, she found the key and unlocked the door. Without turning her head, she said, 'But I'm not in the market for a casual affair.'

'It wouldn't be casual,' he said mildly enough, and when she lifted her astonished face towards him she saw something like amusement glitter in his eyes.

Only it wasn't; her heart quivered in her breast as he smiled down at her with a narrowed intensity.

*Why not?* she thought again, unbearably tempted by a passionate longing that urged her to fling away common sense and accept what he was offering.

Even feverish and barely able to see him, she'd been aware of his potent masculine impact, her body responding instinctively and instantly.

The breath stopped in her throat when she realised that this was already more than simple sexual hunger. Oh, she'd be physically safe, but if she surrendered to this overwhelming need, she'd face a far greater risk—that of losing her heart irretrievably and forever.

The sudden flash of understanding gave her the strength to pull back. Quietly, steadily, she said, 'I don't—I don't think I'm ready for any sort of relationship right now, Kelt.'

It was the first time she'd said his name except in her mind.

He looked at her for too long, his gaze so piercing she had to stop herself from closing her eyes against it, and then he nodded. 'Perhaps it's for the best,' he said with a cool smile. 'And don't let Rosie talk you into any of her mad schemes.'

Aching as though she'd been beaten, Hani went inside while he walked down the path. Later that afternoon, Arthur Wellington drove the car down.

'Before he left, Kelt said to tell you it's fully insured and that you're to use it as much as you like,' he said.

'That's very kind of him.' She didn't have any right to ask where Kelt had gone.

He gave her a thoughtful look. 'He can certainly be kind,' he agreed.

Although the sun shone from a brilliant sky she felt cold and bereft, as though she'd thrown away something of great value.

But she'd have ended up paying a bitter, lifelong price for passion, she thought, trying to fortify her resolve. Because Kelt had offered her nothing beyond that.

Even if he had, she'd have been forced to refuse; it was bitterly ironic that Felipe's death resolved nothing except the fear that had been an ever-present shadow. She couldn't, with honour, return to Moraze or resume her old life.

The thought of media attention filled her with horror. Far better to stay dead.

The next afternoon she drove into town to buy groceries and check Alonso on the internet; although he and his family were easy to find, in all the references and photographs there was nothing that could connect him to Felipe's circle.

But even so, she didn't dare run the risk of him recognising her and remembering her supposed death.

As Gabby played with leaves and spindrift, and made her first forays into the sea, her mistress tried to map out a future.

Without success; her thoughts kept finding their way to Kelt. Unconsciously she'd grown to rely on seeing him, and it was painful to discover just how empty and barren life without him could be.

Her heart felt like a stone in her breast, and her dreams became forlorn affairs of pain and loss and frantic searching, as though some essential part of her was missing.

So when Rosie arrived just after lunch one day she greeted her with real pleasure until she started to discuss her plans for the beach party—plans that involved Hani as guest of honour.

'No,' Hani said firmly.

After her attempts at persuasion had failed, Rosie pulled a face. 'You're just as stubborn as Kelt! He said I wasn't to bother you, and threatened to call the whole thing off if I asked you to do *anything*. All I said was that this beach would be wonderful for the party—it's so pretty and sheltered, and it's great for swimming—but he vetoed that too. And now Alonso's gone back home!'

'Kelt's got this thing about my illness,' Hani offered, so relieved by this that she felt giddy for a moment. At least she wouldn't have to skulk around the bach for three months!

'How are you?' Rosie examined her. 'You look fine— much better than you did the first time I met you, actually.'

'I feel great.' Hani smiled. 'Gabby's seeing to it that I get a fair amount of exercise, and it's so beautiful here. I expected the water to be too cold for me, but I love its briskness.'

'Oh—hasn't Kelt forbidden you to swim alone?' Rosie sounded surprised.

'No.' Paddling was as far as she'd got; she hadn't swum for six years. 'And I doubt if I'd take much notice of him if he did. Why would he do that?'

'His mother drowned while she was swimming on her own off Homestead Bay. He found her body.'

'Oh, how awful,' Hani said involuntarily, repressing memories she tried to keep in the darkest recess of her mind. 'Poor Kelt.'

'Yes. She was a darling.'

The next day, shopping for groceries, Hani realised that the school holidays must have started. The car parks were full and there were children everywhere, fizzing with a palpable air of enjoyment beside their harried parents.

Summer holidays, she thought reminiscently, eyeing a small tot in a frilly sundress with an old-fashioned sun bonnet protecting her freckled face—apparently the latest fashion for under-twos here.

Kelt's words came to her: '—a husband, children…'

By cutting herself off she'd given up any hope of such a future. In fact, she thought now, she'd simply given up hope. Her attempt to kill herself had failed, but in a way she'd committed emotional suicide.

For the first time she appreciated the full impact of the decision she'd made at eighteen. As she was convinced that not only had she failed to live up to her brother's standards, but also that she was a definite threat to him and to the islanders her family had ruled for hundreds of years, the decision had been understandable.

Now she realised that her shamed self-absorption had prolonged Felipe Gastano's power over her. And in a way, her refusal to accept Kelt's delicately worded proposition had been a continuation of that mortification.

But Felipe was dead. Did she dare emerge from her exile and take what she could from life?

Even if it couldn't lead to anything permanent?

Back at the bach she unpacked her purchases and put them away, then took Gabby for a short run, before curling up on a lounger in the sun, the puppy a sleepy little bundle against her bare legs.

'No, no playing,' she said, stroking the soft little ears. 'I have to sort out my thoughts.'

Her gaze drifted to the top of the tree-clad ridge between her little cove and Homestead Bay. Only a few weeks ago her actions had seemed perfectly logical and sensible—until Kelt woke something inside her, a yearning that had turned her life upside down.

'So instead of just reacting,' she told Gabby, 'I need to think this through carefully.'

Except that it was so easy to let her mind drift off into wonderful daydreams. Ruthlessly banishing them, she began to make mental lists.

Surely it would be safe to settle in New Zealand? After all, her qualifications were New Zealand ones; that would help her case. And the charity that ran the school on Tukuulu was based here—maybe they'd organise her a job.

She might even be able to marry...

No, that was just another daydream, a fantasy like her dreams of being a circus rider. Marriage would involve trusting someone with her secrets.

'Stop right there!' she said out loud, astonished by her wayward thoughts.

Gabby woke with a start, and after a lavish yawn that revealed every one of her needle-teeth indicated that she wanted to get down. Once on the ground, she staggered across to drink heartily from her water bowl, then arranged herself in the sun for another nap.

Not marriage—not that. Not ever. Marriage would mean

living a lie, because she couldn't tell Kelt—any prospective husband—about that sordid episode in her past, and her cowardice.

But an affair was a different matter. Excitement beat through Hani—sweet, intense, potent. Softly, her eyes on the little dog, she said aloud, 'I want to know what desire—what passion—is like when there's no hidden agenda, when the emotions are open and honest and not confused with love.'

No marriage, no commitment—just a straightforward, uncomplicated relationship between two people who wanted each other and had no reason not to act on that erotic attraction.

'A thoroughly modern affair,' she said into the heavy air, scented by sun and sea and greenery.

Her breath came faster between her lips, but her voice trailed away. So how did a woman go about indicating to a man—whom she'd already rebuffed—that she wasn't averse to changing her mind?

She had no idea.

But nothing ventured, nothing won.

A large motorboat swung around the headland and roared into the bay, its huge wake creaming the water before crashing into the rocks at the base of each headland.

Gabby woke with a start and let off a couple of startled yaps. 'It's all right,' Hani soothed her, picking her up and holding her in her lap. 'They'll go as soon as they've had a look around.'

But they didn't. A few metres off the beach the engine cut and the anchor rattled down. The silence was broken by loud yells as the people on board—all men, she noted—dived over the side.

With a shock she realised they were naked and the hair on the back of her neck lifted in a primitive intimation of danger.

She bit her lip. No, she was being foolish. Clearly they thought they were alone in the bay, and on such a glorious day, why not swim naked?

She took Gabby inside and tried to read, but while the sun eased down the sky her apprehension grew stronger as she listened to the new arrivals' increasingly raucous yells and laughter.

She'd made up her mind to ring Arthur when she saw a car heading down the drive. With a sigh of relief she went out to the gate.

Her relief turned to joy when she realised that the driver was Kelt. One hand clutching the gatepost, she watched him get out of the big farm vehicle, and her heart expanded within her and soared.

Yes, she thought, giddy with elation, yes, this is what I want. This is right for me now.

The future could look after itself. She might grieve when this was over, but she'd never regret it.

After one searching scrutiny he demanded, 'Have they come ashore?'

'No. No, I'm fine, but I was getting a bit worried.'

He said austerely, 'I've only just got home. Otherwise I'd have been down sooner.'

'They're not actually doing anything I could object to, just making a noise,' she said, adding, 'But I was about to ring. How did you know they were here?'

'I checked the bay when I drove in. I know the owner of the boat; his son and some of his friends—all at university— have been on a cruise around the Bay of Islands, and this is their last night. They're good enough kids, but clearly they've been drinking.' As if it was an afterthought, he went on, 'A lot of deaths at sea are linked to alcohol.'

Of course, his mother had drowned. Quietly Hani asked, 'What can you do?'

'Hail them from the beach, then take them back to the marina.'

Unthinkingly she said, 'How will you get home? Arthur?'

He gave her another keen glance, something kindling in the depths of his eyes that set her pulse dancing. 'Arthur's planning to go out tonight. Why don't you drive to Kaitake and pick me up from there?'

Hani realised that she'd been offered her chance to countermand her rejection. A wild, sweet excitement charged her body with delight. 'Yes, of course.' Before she could say anything else a particularly noisy yell made her glance anxiously over her shoulder. 'But will you be safe? They sound violent.'

'They're just horsing around,' he said with such rock-solid confidence that she almost stopped worrying. 'To be fair, they probably don't know there's someone in residence here.'

Apprehension warred with acceptance. One of the reasons she'd learned to trust Kelt was that sense of responsibility; he wouldn't have been Kelt if he hadn't decided to take them back.

But when he turned to go she grabbed his sleeve. 'Kelt— wait. I don't think—'

He looked down at her. 'Don't worry,' he said calmly. 'I'm not stupid. If I didn't know them I'd get back-up, but they're not bad. Just a bit wild and, at the moment, more than a bit drunk.'

Hani stared at him, then reached up and kissed his mouth. He went rigid, and she was just about to pull back in sick humiliation when he snatched her into his arms and returned the kiss with an uncompromising passion that sent hunger rocketing through her.

Eyes gleaming, he put her away from him and surveyed her with narrowed, glittering eyes. 'You shouldn't do that sort of thing if you don't want to arouse false hopes.'

'I do,' she said, flushing hotly.

'Do what?'

That fierce kiss had unsealed something inside her, let loose a need that ached through her like a sweet fever.

'Do want to arouse,' she repeated, holding his gaze as more colour scorched across her face. 'And the hopes wouldn't be false.'

# CHAPTER ELEVEN

EYES narrowed and intent, Kelt looked down at her. Hani gave him a tremulous, shy smile. He made as if to step towards her, then stopped. His hands clenched at his sides, and he said between his teeth, 'I'll hold you to that.'

Hani's heart pounded, almost blocking out the sound of the waves on the sand. *What had she done?* But it was right; some primal womanly instinct told Hani that if she didn't surrender to this moment, this man, she'd regret it for the rest of her life.

Trying to look cool and sophisticated, she said, 'I'll see you at the marina.'

'It will take the cruiser about half an hour to get there.' He paused another charged moment, then turned and strode off towards the beach without looking back.

Tensely, anxiously, Hani watched him come to a stop just above the tidemark. He didn't have to hail the boat; the men on the cruiser saw him, and after a short shouted exchange of words a small rubber dinghy came hurtling recklessly towards the shore, grounding on the sand with a jerk that almost hurled the driver overboard.

Kelt said something that set the driver laughing as he collected himself. With one strong, sure movement Kelt heaved the dinghy into deeper water, then swung lithely into the craft and took the controls.

Hani relaxed, thinking with a trace of irony that her anxiety had been entirely wasted. But she stayed there, fingers knotted together, her straining gaze fixed on his tall, athletic figure until he climbed into the cruiser. The other men crowded around him, clearly welcoming his arrival. Ten minutes later the anchor rattled up, and the big boat swung smoothly around, a faint wake feathering the water as it made its way out between the tree-clad headlands.

Almost half an hour later to the minute, Hani watched the big cruiser ease into a mooring at the marina. The disembarked sailors were less noisy by now, and became noticeably more subdued when they were met by a man—presumably the owner of the boat. Kelt spoke to him, and the two men shook hands before Kelt started towards her.

Her heart picked up speed again, and her eyes turned hungry. He looked...wonderful. Tall and lithe and—hers. For tonight, anyway.

Oh, she hoped so.

'Everything's OK,' he said briefly as he got into the passenger seat.

Feeling oddly pleased that he trusted her to drive him home, she put the car in gear and concentrated on backing out. 'Obviously you didn't have any trouble with them.'

He looked a trifle surprised. 'Not after I pointed out that by letting me take them back they might—*just*—be trusted to take the cruiser out again, whereas they wouldn't have a show if I had to ring the owner and ask him to come and deal with the situation.'

Her laugh took him by surprise. Low and huskily seductive, it rippled through the car like music. 'You should do that more often,' he said without thinking.

'What? Reverse?'

'Laugh. I don't think I've heard it before.'

What the hell had happened to her? Something so traumatic that it had killed her laughter.

Her sideways glance reminded him of a hunted animal, but her voice was level and cool. 'I'm sure you must have—or am I that glum?'

'I wouldn't describe you as glum.' Look at the road, he told himself. If he kept his eyes off her perhaps he could restrain his reckless hunger, so heady it threatened to unleash the control he'd always kept over himself.

He'd never had any worry about restraint before, but tonight, with Hannah, he'd need to temper his carnal craving. She'd had at least one bad experience; he didn't want to terrify her, or hurt her.

He wanted to make it perfect for her.

She startled him by saying, 'If I haven't laughed in the time you've known me I must be lousy company.'

'Fishing?' he asked laconically, because talking nonsense might help. 'You must realise that I find your company extremely—stimulating. Your laughter was worth the wait.'

More than anything—even more than satisfying the carnal hunger that prowled through him—he wanted to hear her laugh again.

Fiercely Hani concentrated on driving. His words twisted her heart, adding something vital to the purely physical charge between them.

If she kept on this way, she thought in a sudden panic, she might end up loving him, a willing prisoner of desire.

She didn't dare.

She just didn't have the courage to open her heart again, to accept the possibility—no, she admitted starkly, the *inevitability*—of pain.

About to tell him she couldn't go through with it, she clamped her lips together. Don't dress this up as love, she advised herself trenchantly. You did that once before, and look where it got you...

Think of making love to Kelt as medicine you have to take to get well again.

Nice medicine...

And could have laughed at the banality of her thoughts. Making love to Kelt would be a sensuous, mind-blowing delight, nothing like medicine.

And she was going to do it because she'd let Felipe's brutality crush her instincts for far too long. But more—oh, so much more, some hidden part of her jeered—because she *wanted* Kelt. Wanted him so much she could actually taste the longing on her tongue; she ached with it, afire with the hunger that now seemed so normal, so natural. Anticipation ran hotly through her, melting her racing, tumbled thoughts, her inhibitions in a flood of hungry desire.

She said, 'I'll see to it that I laugh more, then.'

'I'll look forward to it,' he told her with a narrow smile that made her concentrate on keeping her breath steady.

The rest of the trip home was conducted in almost complete silence.

*Home?* she thought in bewilderment, shocked at the mental slip. Moraze had always been her one true home, but somehow this beautiful, peaceful place had become precious.

Slowing down as they approached the turn-off to his house, she said, 'Oh, I forgot. Your car is at the bach.' She flashed him a glance. 'Would you like to stay to dinner?'

She didn't dare look at him again during the short silence before he said, 'Thank you, yes. I need a shower, so drop me off here and I'll walk down.'

Obediently she did that, saying just as he got out, 'I've already made chilli, but I like it hot. If you don't I can make something else, although it won't be meat.'

'Don't worry, I like it hot too,' he said, his cool tone very much at variance with the dark gleam in his eyes.

Hani drove off, wondering what on earth had pushed her into that invitation. A weak effort to give their lovemaking some context, a feeble pretence that it meant more than a soulless connection of bodies?

Probably, she thought, but at least this time she knew what she was doing.

Gabby greeted her with joy from amidst a newspaper in shreds over the sitting-room floor. Laughing, Hani cleared it up, took the pup for a short walk outside, then hurried through the shower and into a sunfrock with a pretty little bolero to cover her upper arms as the sun went down.

As she took the chilli from the fridge she wondered whether she should try to reduce its bite. Well, she had a large pot of New Zealand's superb yoghurt and some coriander. If Kelt burnt his mouth he could ease it with that.

With it she'd serve rice and a large green salad, followed by strawberries and the yoghurt. A bubble of anticipation expanded in her stomach.

But she had no wine. After a moment she shrugged. It wasn't necessary, and besides, wine and chilli didn't always go well together. Anyway, she didn't need alcohol; she was half-intoxicated already, as though the very best French champagne were circulating through her veins.

When Kelt came in through the door the feeling of delirious lightness morphed into something darker, more potent. Deep inside her a smouldering erotic hunger blazed into desperate life at the hard-honed angles of his handsome face, the air of power and command that controlled his compelling masculinity.

In a raw voice he said, 'I brought some champagne, but I don't need it. Just looking at you is enough to make me drunk.'

Hani had no idea what to say. Unevenly she finally managed, 'Put it in the fridge.'

She'd imagined them sitting outside as the sun sank over the hills, talking a little, but suddenly she felt she couldn't wait. Trying to hide the heady clamour of desire, she stirred the chilli, but when the silence stretched too far she had to glance up.

He was still watching her, his eyes narrowed and intent, his mouth a hard, straight line.

Hunger tore at her. Smiling tremulously, she put the spoon down.

He took a step towards her before stopping to say in a thick, driven voice, 'I'm not going to touch you. Not yet.'

Something splintered into shards of sensation inside her. In a tone she didn't recognise she said, 'In that case, do you mind if I touch you?'

'Hannah,' he said, and then with a tight, humourless laugh, 'No, you should be Honey. It suits you much better. Warm and golden and sweet—you've been tormenting me ever since I saw you. Once you touch me I doubt very much if I'll be responsible for anything that happens.'

Dazzled by the thought of affecting him so strongly, she came slowly towards him, eyes darkening as she took in the control he was exerting, the clenched hands, his waiting, predatory stillness.

She should be afraid, she thought exultantly, but she wasn't scared of Kelt.

Hands behind her back, she stood on tiptoe and kissed the tanned hollow of his throat. He made a muffled sound and his arms came around her, pulling her against him so hard she could feel every rigid muscle, the powerful male strength he was keeping in check, the rapid uneven pounding of his heart—and the hunger that met and matched hers.

And then he lifted her, and she remembered how amazingly safe she'd always felt in his arms. Hers tightened around his neck as he shouldered through the door into the bedroom and across to the big bed, sitting her down on the side with a gentleness that reassured every drifting, hardly recognised fear.

He dropped a swift, famished kiss on her throat, then straightened, looking down at her with a glitter in his eyes that set her pulses racing so fast she thought she might faint with anticipation.

'I don't even dare undress you,' he said with a taut smile. 'I might tear this pretty thing, and that would be a shame.'

He was talking, she realised, to ease the tension that gripped them both. A swift relief swept over her at his understanding. In a soft, low voice she said, 'Then perhaps we should undress ourselves.'

'An excellent idea.' He stepped back and his hands went to the opening of his shirt.

Fascinated, she watched his lean fingers flick open the buttons to reveal the broad chest beneath, his powerful muscles emphasised by a scroll of hair across the sleek, tanned skin. Excitement clamoured through Hani, a fierce demand she'd never known before.

When he'd shrugged out of his shirt she said on a sharp, indrawn breath, 'You are—magnificent.'

'Thank you.' One black brow rose when she continued drinking him in.

Flushing, she pulled off her tiny bolero, revealing her bare shoulders. Heat kindled in the cold blue flames of his eyes, but he made no move towards her as she eased the sundress over her head.

Too shy to let it drop to the floor, she let it hang loosely in front of her. Dry-throated, she said, 'I think it must be your turn.'

He removed his shoes and socks, then let his trousers drop to the floor.

Hani dragged a startled breath into empty lungs. Long legs, strongly muscled from riding, narrow hips, and he was— big, she thought, her eyes darting from the sole part of his anatomy that was still clothed.

'May I?'

Closing her eyes for a second, she nodded, opening them only when he'd taken her dress from her nerveless fingers and put it on the chair beside the bed.

Clad only in one small scrap of cotton, she had never felt so naked.

Harshly he said, 'You are utterly beautiful.'

And for him she felt beautiful. With a trembling smile she held out her arms, and he came down beside her with a rush, tumbling her backwards so that her breasts were exposed and open to his eager mouth.

But first he kissed her lips—tender, quick kisses that stoked the fires between her loins unbearably. Then he possessed himself of her mouth, plunging deep in an imitation of the most intimate embrace of all. Almost immediately she shuddered with hunger, her straining body afire against the hard, potent length of his, her breath coming in short, hoarse pants, her eyes wild as she stared up into his face.

Hani expected him to take her there and then, but instead he kissed her breasts, made himself master of her body, caressing with his hands and his tongue so that her every cell recognised and responded to his touch.

And he gave her the freedom to do the same to him until she learned intimately the swell of muscle and line of sinew, the fine matte texture of his skin, the contrast with the scrolls of hair across his chest, the way his body tensed beneath her seeking hands...

Frantic, driven by a voluptuous desire, a longing so desperate all her fears disappeared, she pulled at him, her hands tightening across the sleek skin of his back, her voice urgent and importunate.

Until at last he moved over her and with one smooth, easy thrust took her.

Every muscle in Hani's body contracted, welcoming him, clinging to him, beginning an involuntary, automatic rhythm that soared higher and higher into a place she'd never known, so when at last the climax overwhelmed her in delight and ecstasy she cried out and surrendered completely.

Only to be hurled further into that unknown rapture when he joined her there, his big body tense and bowed, his head flung back. Locked in erotic union, they reached that place together, and eventually came down together, slick bodies relaxing, their hearts slowing into a normal rhythm until Kelt turned to catch her in his arms again and pull her against him.

He kissed her wordless murmur into silence, and said against her lips, 'Tired?'

'Mmm,' she said, and he laughed, and held her while she slid into sleep unlike anything she'd ever known before.

It was dark when she woke, and she knew instantly that he was awake. She was sprawled across him, her head pillowed on one shoulder, her hair streaming across his chest.

He must have sensed her wakening, because he said, 'It's almost midnight.'

'Oh, lord,' she said, suffused with guilt, 'and I haven't fed you! How long have you been awake?'

'Long enough.' He dropped a kiss on the top of her head.

'Long enough for what?'

The silence was so short she thought it hadn't happened until he drawled wickedly, 'To work up an appetite.'

She spluttered into laughter, and hurtled off the bed. 'Then we'd better eat that dinner—if it's still edible,' she said, climbing into her dressing gown.

Smiling, he got up, and together they ate, took Gabby out, and drank a little champagne, only to leave it unfinished when desire overpowered them once more.

Hani slept again, but woke to tears aching behind her eyes, tears that spilled across Kelt's chest. Grateful that he stayed asleep, she surrendered to bitter-sweet joy. In his arms she'd found true fulfilment, and now she knew that when this interlude was over she'd spend the rest of her life longing for him.

But she had never been so happy. Making love with Kelt had been—amazing and wonderful and glorious and sensuous and...just plain *magnificent*.

Just as amazing was that she hadn't thought of Felipe once.

For the first time she felt well and truly loved in every respect.

Except the emotional, she realised as days and nights passed in a voluptuous feast for all her senses—a dazzling, mind-blowing parade of sensuousness in which Kelt taught her just how wonderful making love could be.

Each day she fell deeper and deeper into love—and knew with a hopeless hunger that Kelt didn't love her. Although he showed her he could be tender and generous as well as passionate and demanding, she sensed an unbridged distance between them.

She didn't ask for anything more; she even tried to convince herself that she was well content. But as the summer lazed on, she found herself wondering if perhaps—just perhaps—they might some time cross the invisible, unspoken boundaries they'd set on their affair.

Daydreaming again…

One evening, coming back into the bay after a picnic on a tiny offshore island, he asked, 'It's over six weeks since you had that bout of fever.'

Hani trailed her hand in the water and frowned as she counted the days. 'So it is.' She watched him rowing the old wooden dinghy, letting her eyes drift meaningfully over his shoulders, the muscles bunching with each smooth flick of the oars. 'I've been occupied with other things,' she said sweetly, and flicked some water his way.

He grinned. 'Mind over matter?'

'Or the placebo effect.'

He laughed, his eyes gleaming. 'Perhaps there's something to it. We could get all scientific about this; I have to go away in three days' time, so we could see whether you keep count of the time while I'm away.'

Lost in the wonder of being his lover, Hani had to bite her tongue to stop herself from asking him where he was going.

'I'll be away about ten days,' he said calmly. 'I'd ask you to come with me—'

Before he could come up with whatever excuse, she shook her head and interrupted. 'No.' Her heart twisted. Not ever.

She hurried on, 'As for the fever, I think it's gone. I feel—strong, somehow. Good.'

The dinghy grounded on the sand and things went on exactly the same—at least, that was what Hani told herself. But for the three days she found herself tensing whenever he came, almost as though she had to extract every ounce of pleasure, commit to memory every tiny alteration in his deep voice, the way his smile melted her bones—even the exact shade of his eyes, so close to the border between blue and steel-grey that it was impossible to state categorically what colour they were...

And that, she thought robustly, was stupid. He'd only be away for a week and a half.

The days dragged. Oh, she had the delicious memories of the night before he'd left when he'd made love to her as though—as though he wasn't coming back, she thought, trying to laugh at herself.

But memories weren't enough. She wanted Kelt. No, worse than that—she *needed* him.

The night before he was due back restlessness and an oppressive cloud of foreboding drove her to seek refuge from her own thoughts and longings, and she sat with Gabby in her lap—a bigger and more sturdy puppy now, showing every sign of developing a strong character. The soft, warm weight comforted her a little, but she longed to see Kelt again, to tell him...what?

*I love you?* 'Not likely,' she said forlornly, and got up and turned off the television.

Later, she heard the low sound of a car come down the hill. She began to shake, then got to her feet and walked carefully to the door, opening it as Kelt raised his hand to knock.

His face was drawn, but he was smiling. Every cell in her body recognised him with joyous outcry. Holding out her hands, she drew him in with her and lifted her face in mute invitation.

He kissed her with a famished intensity that banished every last inhibition. When at last he lifted his head, she said, 'You were away nine days, eleven hours and forty-three minutes.'

'I know.' His eyes gleamed with sensuous amusement. 'And every one of them dragged.'

'I know.' She laughed softly, huskily, and kissed his throat. 'Food first?'

*Or do you want to go straight to bed?*

Her unspoken question astonished her. How had she summoned the courage to be so—so brazen?

A darting look up from beneath her lashes revealed the strong framework of his face, as though the tanned skin had tightened over it.

And his voice was raw when he said, 'If you keep that up we won't make it to the bed.'

Boldly she lifted her head and kissed his chiselled mouth, then outlined it with the tip of her tongue. His heart thudded against her, strong and fast. Heat bloomed her skin, and she could have breathed in the faint, elusive male scent of him, tangy and arousing, for the rest of her life.

'That would probably shock Gabby,' she murmured. And added, because she had to, 'You guessed I'd had a bad experience. It's—finished with, Kelt. I'm not afraid any more.'

He looked down at her, eyes narrowed into blazing slits, so piercing she could hardly meet his gaze. 'You're sure?'

'Completely sure.' And to seal it she initiated another kiss, one that was frankly voracious, showing him just how much she wanted him.

This time he returned it—with interest—before sweeping her up in his arms and carrying her once more into the bedroom.

This time—oh, this time there was none of the practised gentleness she'd come to expect. Kelt made love to her as though he'd spent just as many lonely night hours longing for her as she had for him, as though they were lovers separated by years that had only whetted their desire, once more together.

Glorying in his ardour, she allowed her needs and desires free rein, responding to each kindling caress, each sensuously tormenting kiss, with everything she was, everything she felt.

And although their lovemaking was fast and fierce, when that moment of release came again it threw her even higher as wave after wave of pleasure surged through her, sending her to that rapturous place where desire and satisfaction melded into mutual bliss.

Much later, safe in his arms, she accepted that she loved him. And that it didn't matter. The sheer grandeur of her feelings for him outweighed the knowledge of pain to come, when she left him.

She murmured, 'You were away too long.'

'I won't need to go back to Carathia for a while,' he said calmly.

'Carathia?' She yawned. 'Isn't that a little country on the edge of the Adriatic? What were you doing there?'

'I was there on business, but in the end I helped my brother put down a rebellion,' he said dryly.

Love-dazed, her tired mind barely registered the words, but when they sank in she sat up and stared down at him, her heart shaking inside her at the sight of him, long and lean and tanned against the white sheets.

He was smiling, without humour, and his eyes were sombre.

'What? *What* did you say?' she spluttered.

'My brother is the ruler of Carathia.' His expression hardened. 'I went there because there was a spot of bother, and he needed me.' He smiled and pulled her down again, kissing the swell of her breast. 'Mmm,' he murmured against her skin, 'you smell delicious. I sometimes think it's what I miss most about you.'

Little tremors of sensation raced through her, urgently and pleading. Ignoring them, she whispered, 'What do you mean—the ruler?'

The children on the beach had called Kelt the Duke, and talked of a grandmother who wore a crown. Oh, God, why hadn't she listened? Why hadn't she asked?

Kelt turned her face up so that he could see it, and a frown drew his black brows together. 'My brother, Gerd, is the new Grand Duke of Carathia.'

Dreams Hani hadn't even recognised crashed around her. Unbeknown to herself she must have been fantasising—*hoping?*—that somehow, she might be able to forge some sort of connection with Kelt. That with him she'd be able to make a life here in this enchanted place.

That perhaps there might be a future for them if she could trust him enough to be able to tell him about herself and her past.

'I didn't know,' she said in a stunned voice. 'No one told me.' No one but the children...

'Most people around here are aware of it; my grandparents used to come and stay here on occasion, and my brother and I spent all our holidays here.' He finished coolly, 'It's no big deal.'

Hani turned to hide her head in his chest. His casual words had killed every inchoate, wordless hope. She didn't dare have any sort of relationship with a man whose wealth and good looks and ancient heritage made him food for gossip mills. Even as his mistress she'd shame him—she cringed, thinking of the way the tabloids would treat her reappearance.

Kelt asked, 'What is it? Tell me.'

'I didn't know,' she said faintly. And because she couldn't tell him what that knowledge had done to her, she asked, 'But why do you live here—in New Zealand?'

He shrugged, and his arms tightened around her. She lay with her face against his heart, listening to the slowing beat, inhaling his beloved scent, and felt her world crumble around her again, her splintered hopes painfully stabbing her.

'It's no big deal,' he said again casually. 'Our grandparents met while my grandmother was fighting a nasty little rebellion amongst the mountain people, one fomented by her sister. Our grandfather was a New Zealander, and he saved her life in an ambush. Kiwinui was his heritage, just as it's been mine. They were married, and had one son. Our mother was a Greek princess. We spent quite a lot of time here as children. My brother has always known he'd be Grand Duke one day. I've always preferred New Zealand.'

Hani sensed that he wasn't telling her everything, but she didn't dare speak. Instead she nodded, letting loose a swathe of black hair across his skin. Their hips met, moved together with sensuous languor, and she felt him stir against her.

Tomorrow, she thought weakly. She would steal one more night of paradise in his arms, and tomorrow she'd tell him that it was over.

# CHAPTER TWELVE

HANI woke, to find Kelt, fully clothed, bending over her. She smiled and he bent and kissed her.

Against his lips she murmured, 'What…?'

'I am expecting a call from Gerd,' he told her. Then he smiled, and said in a warmer voice, 'Go back to sleep.'

But by then she'd remembered, and her eyes were agonised when he turned and walked out of the door into the half-light of dawn.

When the sound of his vehicle had died away she got up and put Gabby outside. A sliver of golden light against the horizon heralded another summer day, but in her heart it would always be winter.

Dragging her footsteps like an old woman, she walked into the bedroom, Gabby gambolling at her heels. She had to get out of here, before he came back. She'd take the car into Kaitake and catch a bus to—to anywhere. No, to Auckland, because it was big enough to get lost in. She'd leave Gabby with plenty of water and food and ring tonight to make sure they knew she was there. She wasn't worried about getting Kelt; Arthur answered the phone at the homestead.

She'd leave Kelt a note. Feverishly she started composing it in her mind: *It's been great, but I have to go—thank*

*you so much for all you've done for me. Please look after
Gabby for me…*

He'd never know just how much he had done for her. Making
love with him had wiped the tainted memories of the past,
leaving her whole again and stronger than she'd ever been.

'No,' she said out loud, startling herself. 'No, he deserves
better than a stupid note.'

Last time she'd run without telling anyone it had been for
her life. This time it would be sheer cowardice. She wouldn't
leave Kelt without an explanation of why she had to go.
Although it would be savagely painful and embarrassing to
tell him that she suspected she was falling in love with him,
she could at least salvage some sort of honour.

By lunchtime her suitcase was packed and she'd rung for
the bus timetable, and was taking the coach that came through
later in the afternoon.

A knock on the door froze her into place. She didn't need
Gabby's happy little greeting to tell her who it was. I'm not ready,
she thought, panic-stricken, knowing she'd never be ready.

Dragging a deep breath into her compressed lungs, she
came out of the bedroom and closed the door behind her.

Gabby was prancing around the door, her tail wagging.
White-faced, Hani opened the door to Kelt, who took one look
at her and demanded, 'What the hell is the matter?'

Before she had time to think, she blurted, 'I have something to tell you.'

His eyes hardened, but he came in and closed the door
behind him. 'Are you sure? It's early days yet, but don't worry.
We'll get married.'

Hani's heart gave a great leap, then settled like a lead
weight in her chest. Retreating a few paces, she said, 'I'm not
pregnant.' Pain stabbed her, sharp and brutal.

His brows drew together and she saw the warrior, angular and relentless. 'All right, what is it?'

'I'll be leaving soon,' she said quietly. 'I just wanted you to know that you've made me very happy and I'll always remember you.'

His eyes narrowed. In a silky voice he said, 'If that's so, why are you going? And before you say anything, I know you love me, so it has to be something else.'

Hani stared at him. 'How arrogant you are,' she said, but the spark had gone from her voice and she had to force herself to meet that merciless gaze. 'We made love, that's all. There's a difference.'

A cold kick of fear silenced her as she watched his hands clench into fists by his sides. 'Is that all it was?' he asked in a voice like molten metal. He smiled, and came towards her, and for the first time ever she felt truly afraid of him.

Yet she didn't flinch when he raised his hands and his fingers settled gently around the golden column of her throat. He was so close she could see the pulse beating in his jaw, smell the hot, primal scent that was his alone; if she lifted the hand that itched to move of its own accord, she'd feel the heat of his fine-grained skin against her fingertips.

And she'd melt in abject surrender.

He said softly, 'How could it be so unimportant when it made you cry? That first night—you thought I was asleep, but I heard you, felt the hot tears soak into my skin, and I knew then that whatever you felt for me wasn't something you'd ever forget.'

*Do it now. Make it clear.* Head held high, she met his narrowed gaze and said coolly, 'I had issues from the past. You showed me how unimportant they were. I'll always be grateful to you for that.'

'I don't believe you,' he said between his teeth. 'Tell me the truth, Hannah.'

If she did he'd despise her. Dumbly she stared up into icy eyes.

His fingers smoothed over the rapidly beating pulse at the base of her throat, then he dropped his hands and stepped back, smiling without humour. 'So you've had your *past issues*—' he said the words with caustic emphasis '—resolved by extremely good sex, and now you're leaving, no bones broken, no hearts cracked.'

Instantly Hani felt cold, abandoned. She owed him the truth. In a low, shamed voice, she said, 'Why didn't you tell me you weren't what I thought you were, an ordinary New Zealand farmer—?'

'I *am* a New Zealand farmer—'

'You're much more than that. Your grandmother is a grand duchess, and you are not only rich, you're also hugely powerful. You must have known I didn't know.'

'Oddly enough,' he said in a caustic voice, 'I found your attitude interesting, and very refreshing. But what difference does any of that make?'

She braced herself. 'A lot. You really don't know anything about me. I'm afraid I've lied to you again and again.' It took all of her courage to go on, but she had to make him understand. 'Starting with my name. It's neither Hannah nor Honey. Until six years ago I was Hani de Courteville, and my brother was Rafiq de Courteville, the ruler of Moraze.'

'Moraze?' She watched as his keen mind processed the information and slotted it into place. His lashes drooped. 'Go on.'

Everything about him—tone, stance, the formidable intensity of his gaze—was intimidating, but he didn't seem shocked. In fact, she thought wonderingly, her revelation seemed to have confirmed something he'd already suspected.

A small warmth of hope gave her the impetus to continue.

'I spent my childhood there, and went to boarding-school in England, and then to a French university. I was eighteen, and too young—too stupid—to be let loose.' She took another agonising breath. 'My brother organised a chaperone-cum-companion for me, who introduced me to a man called Felipe Gastano. He said he was a French count; later I found out that it was his half-brother who had been born to the title. Unfortunately the brother died conveniently from a drug overdose not long before I met Gastano.'

'Keep going,' Kelt ordered, his gaze never wavering.

She looked down at her hands. The knuckles were white and she was holding herself so stiffly her spine ached. 'He was enormous fun and possessed great charm. I won't bore you with details of our affair; it began with me convinced I had found the man I wanted to marry, and ended when I tried to commit suicide, and only failed by good luck. Or bad luck, as I thought it at the time.'

He said something in a lethal voice, then in a totally different tone, 'My poor girl.' And then his voice changed. 'So why do you plan to leave?'

She could have held out against his anger; that flash of tenderness struck home like an arrow.

In a thin thread of a voice Hani said, 'Felipe introduced me to drugs. I know now that he did it quite deliberately. By the time I decided to commit suicide I was an addict and in desperate trouble.' She didn't dare look at him. 'Felipe intended to take over Moraze and use it as a depot to ship drugs to Europe.'

'How?' Kelt demanded forcefully. 'Your brother would never have allowed that.'

'I was the lever, the hold Felipe would have had over Rafiq. And he—Rafiq—was the lever Felipe used on me.'

A flash of fury in the steel-blue eyes was swiftly extinguished, but she felt it emanating from him, fiercely controlled but violent. Before he could speak she hurried on, 'I told him I was leaving him, but he threatened to have Rafiq killed if I did.'

'Go on,' Kelt said evenly.

She could read nothing—neither condemnation nor sympathy in his expression. Chilled, she forced herself to continue, 'I knew then that the only thing I could do was die. But not before I'd written to Rafiq, telling him what Felipe planned to do. Then I went to a small Mediterranean island where Rafiq and I had holidayed once. I just walked into the water, and it was such a relief when I finally gave up swimming and surrendered to the sea.'

She could see the rigid control he was exerting, and some part of her was warmed by it.

'So how did you survive?'

'I don't know,' she said simply. 'I lost consciousness, but before I could drown a fisherman found me.'

Kelt said through his teeth, 'You should have told your brother what had happened to you—he wouldn't have blamed you.'

She gave a bleak, cynical smile. 'Perhaps I should have, but I was an addict. They don't make sensible decisions.' And she'd been so bitterly ashamed. She still was.

'So why did the fisherman not turn you over to the authorities?'

'He was a smuggler, but he was a kind man. He dragged me into his boat and took me to his family. I pleaded with them not to tell anyone where I was.'

'So you could have another go at killing yourself?' he demanded harshly.

'At first,' she admitted, pale and cold under his implacable gaze. 'His wife and mother nursed me through the aftermath of drug addiction, and they all kept quiet about the fact that I'd survived. I owe my life and my sanity to them, and although I was sure I'd never, ever be happy again, they made me promise not to try to kill myself. They said I owed them that, as they'd saved me.' She gave a pale smile. 'The grand-mother told me I had to live so that I could make amends for what I'd done.'

In a voice she'd never heard him use before Kelt said, 'I'd like to meet that family. But I would like even more to meet this Gastano.'

'You can't—he's dead; I searched for him on the internet that day in Kaitake. It's horrible—wicked—to be glad a man is dead, but I am.' At least Kelt and Rafiq were safe now. 'Felipe didn't kill people himself—he ordered others to do it, and it would have been done.' She shivered. 'Even a puppy he bought for me—once he asked me to do something—' She stopped, unable to go on.

'What exactly did he want from you?' Kelt's voice lifted every tiny hair on her body in a reflex old as time.

She'd started this; she had to finish it. 'I'd agreed to go out to lunch with a friend from school. Felipe didn't want me to go, but I made a feeble attempt at asserting my independence and went anyway. He got his chauffeur to kill the puppy while I was away.'

'What happened to him?' Kelt's voice was corrosive.

'Felipe must have tried to use Moraze anyway, because he was killed there in a shoot-out with the military. I suppose he thought that even without me to use as a hostage he could force Rafiq to obey him.' She said in a shaking voice, 'He didn't know Rafiq, of course.'

'When you found out this Gastano was dead, why didn't you let your brother know you were alive?'

'I am ashamed,' she said in a low, shaking voice. 'There are people who know what I was reduced to—who know about me. Young Alonso de Porto, for one.'

'You were targeted and preyed upon,' he said between his teeth. 'Who cares about them?'

'If only you were an ordinary New Zealand farmer it wouldn't really matter,' she said passionately, dark eyes begging him to understand, her voice completely flat, without hope. 'But you're not—you are rich, you have royal links and if we…if we continue our affair, it would soon turn up in the tabloids and then—I'd be found again!'

'Why is that a problem?' he asked relentlessly.

Hani was wringing her hands. Forcing them into stillness, she took several deep breaths and looked him straight in the eye. 'You deserve better than to be embroiled in such a scandal.'

It was impossible to read his face when he demanded, 'Do you love me?'

Don't do this, her heart whispered. She hesitated, huge, imploring eyes fixed on his face. 'I—' She swallowed, unable to say the words. Why wasn't he satisfied with what she'd already told him? Did he want her heart on a plate?

Ruthlessly he said, 'I didn't think you were a coward. Do you love me, Hani?'

Hani flinched. The sound of her real name was inexpressibly sweet on his tongue. 'Think of the uproar if it ever got out that I am alive and was your mistress! Like Rafiq and his family—his wife and two little boys—you'd be shamed in the eyes of the world.'

Willing him to understand, she gazed at him pleadingly, but his expression was controlled, all violence leashed. 'Answer my question.'

Something in his tone alerted Gabby, who stretched elaborately and climbed out of her basket, fussily pacing across to sit on Hani's feet, where she indulged in a good scratch.

Hani hesitated again, her breath knotting in her throat.

'One simple word,' Kelt said inflexibly. 'Either yes or no.'

'I'm afraid,' she whispered.

'I know. But you have to say it.'

She licked her lips. 'I—oh, you know the answer!'

'Tell me.'

Tears magnified her eyes. He didn't come near her, but she could feel him willing her to answer. And from somewhere she found the courage. Unable to bear looking at him, she said in a muffled voice, 'Yes. Yes, of course I love you. I would die for you. But I couldn't bear it if you were humiliated or hurt or made a laughing stock because I was stupidly naïve and—'

'Very young,' he said, and at last came across and took her into his strong embrace.

'But once people know who I am, the whole sordid story will be in every tabloid, and people will sneer at you.' She stared up into his dark, beloved face, then grabbed his arms in desperation and tried to shake some sense into him. It was like trying to move a rock. 'Have you thought of that?'

He asked, 'Have you ever been tempted to use drugs again?'

'Oh, no.' Near to breaking, she shuddered. 'No, not ever again. That was why I came down with such a bad case of fever—I don't like taking anything in case I become addicted.'

'Then you can chalk the whole hideous experience up to youthful folly.'

Unevenly she said, 'Kelt, it's not so simple. What will your brother think?'

He gave her a little shake and said, 'Look at me.'

Slowly, not daring to hope, she lifted her eyes.

Speaking firmly, he said, 'I don't care what Gerd or anyone

else thinks. I'm not going to let you spend the rest of your life expiating sins you didn't commit. You were young, and you were deliberately targeted by an evil man.'

She had to make him see sense. 'Rafiq,' she said urgently. 'My brother—'

Frowning, he interrupted, 'If it had been your brother this had happened to, would you turn away from him?'

More tears ached behind her eyes. 'Of course not,' she said quickly, 'but—'

'I understand why you had to escape, but that reason no longer applies,' Kelt said, his calm tone somehow reinforcing his words. He paused and let her go, taking a step backwards and leaving her alone and cold and aching with love.

When she said nothing, he went on, 'It comes down to one thing only; either you join me in my life and trust me to look after you and our children—stop shaking your head, of course we'll have children!—or I will simply have to kidnap you and keep you here, chained to my side.'

Colour came and went in her skin, and a wild, romantic hope warred with fear. She stared at him, saw uncompromising resolve in his expression, in the straight line of his beautiful mouth, and although her heart quailed joy fountained up through her.

'You're a hard man,' she said, her voice shaking. 'And I love you. But I can't, Kelt. I don't—I just don't have the courage.'

'You had the courage to tell your brother what was going on, to try to sacrifice yourself for him and your country, to hide to keep them safe. You have the courage to do this.'

Her breath caught in her throat. 'You make me out to be more than I am.'

'You are much more than that, my valiant warrior, and I look forward to a long life together so I can convince you of that. I don't blame you for not wanting your story blazed across the media, but it can be managed. I can protect you, and together we'll stare the world down.' Then he smiled, and her heart melted. 'So, can you take that last step and tell me where you'd like to live?'

Hani drew in a sobbing breath and surrendered. He hadn't said anything yet about loving her, but she didn't care. As long as he wanted her she would treasure each day she spent with him.

'I'll live wherever you are,' she told him quietly, her gaze never leaving his beloved face. 'Because if I don't, I won't really be living at all—just existing, as I have been for years. But—could it be here? I love this place.'

This time the loving was different. She expected—longed for—a wild triumph from him, but he was all tenderness, a gentle lovemaking that was strangely more erotic than anything they'd shared before, spun out so long that she lost her composure completely and gave him everything he wanted, demanded everything from him.

And when it was over he cradled her into his lean body and said against her forehead, 'I love you. I want you to marry me as soon as you can organise a wedding.'

Astounded, Hani stared up at him. 'All right,' she whispered, then wept into his shoulder.

'I didn't know,' she finally muttered when he'd mopped her up.

'That I love you?' His voice was harsh, raw with an emotion she had to accept. 'Of course I love you. I've loved you ever since I saw you. Never doubt me.' He paused, his face hardening, and said, 'But before we marry, you need to get in touch with your brother.'

'I—' She froze. 'Oh, God,' she whispered, her throat closing.

'You know you must,' he said quietly. 'I intend to show the world that, whatever happened in the past, I'm not ashamed of loving you. I want to flaunt this precious gift I've been given, and I can't do that if you insist on hiding away like a criminal. You can do it. You're no longer the terrified girl who tried to kill herself and then had to run, and I'll be with you.'

She dragged in a shivering breath. Like this, skin to skin, the sound of his heart in her ears, his body lithe and powerful against her, here in his arms, she could be brave.

And his words had made her think; she would never have turned away from her brother.

'How can Rafiq forgive me for everything I did?' she asked in a muffled voice. 'Most of all for my cowardly silence, allowing him to think I was dead, after the suicide attempt.'

'You'd forgive him.'

'Rafiq would never be so weak—so stupid. He is strong.'

'So are you,' Kelt said, his voice very tender. 'And you're no longer the green girl he once knew—you've grown and matured and gained self-command.'

She looked up into his beloved face. 'And if I don't do this I'll be letting Felipe win.'

He nodded, holding her eyes with his. If Rafiq rejected her she'd be devastated, but she wouldn't be alone. Not any more.

Capitulating, she dragged in another shuddering breath. 'Then I'll go to Moraze.'

'I'll come with you.'

Thirty-six hours later she was walking down the steps of the private jet Kelt had chartered, her knees shaking so badly she didn't dare look around the international airport at Moraze. Kelt slung an arm around her shoulders.

'Relax,' he said calmly. 'Everything will be all right.'

'I know.'

An hour previously she'd rung Rafiq's personal number, and the memory of that conversation was seared in her brain. He had organised for them to land in the military area and a helicopter was standing by to take them to the *castello*.

Sitting tensely in the chopper as it approached the grey castle that once kept watch over the approach to Moraze's harbour, she clutched Kelt's hand.

'It will be all right,' he repeated calmly, sliding his arm around her.

'I c-can't—he *cried*, Kelt. He *cried* when I convinced him that I am alive.'

He kissed her into quietness. 'Of course,' he said. 'If I had a dearly loved sister returned to me from the dead I'd weep too.'

Fortified by her love and Kelt's unfailing support, she no longer automatically assumed every man was like Felipe Gastano, but this startled her into silence.

'I should have met you six years ago,' she said forlornly, then added, 'No, I was too young. Tukuulu taught me things I'll never forget—that I can survive on my own, that I can do work that is worthwhile, that there are people infinitely worse off than I could ever be, and that people are basically the same the world over. I grew up there.'

She wore sunglasses, keeping them on even when the servant—someone she didn't know—ushered them through the *castello*. Kelt's steady hand at her elbow gave her comfort and resolve.

The servant opened the door into Rafiq's study. Her brother was standing by the window, but he turned to look across the room as she took off her sunglasses and produced a wobbly smile for him.

'I'm so sorry,' she said uncertainly. 'So sorry I let you down, and so very sorry I let you believe I was dead.'

He still said nothing, and she went on in a muted voice, 'You see, I thought then it—it was best.'

He came towards her then, his handsome face set in lines that showed her how much control he was exerting. In their shared language he said quietly, 'I have always blamed myself for letting you go without a proper person to look after you.' He held out his arms.

With a choked little cry she ran into them, and for long moments he held her, gently rocking her as she wept on his shoulder.

At last, when she was more composed, he held her away from him and said in English, 'You were always beautiful, but you are radiant now.' His green eyes flicked from her face to that of the man watching them. 'So, having had you restored to me, I understand I am to lose you again? Introduce your man to me.'

Much later, when she and Kelt were alone on the terrace in the shade of the starflower tree, with the moon shining kindly down onto a silver lagoon, he asked, 'All demons slain now?'

'Yes, thank God,' she said soberly, so happy that it hurt. 'When Rafiq told me that everyone in Felipe's organisation was either dead or in prison, I felt a weight roll off my back.'

'I can't help but wish I'd had some hand in Gastano's death,' Kelt said evenly.

She shivered. 'He was an evil man, and nobody will be sorry he's dead.'

'Those who live by death and treachery, die that way,' Kelt said, his tone ruthless.

She was silent for a few moments, then turned and looked up into his face. Kelt could be hard and she suspected that he could be even more dangerous than Felipe had ever been, yet he'd shown her tenderness unsurpassed, and understanding and love.

Stumbling, her words low and intense, she tried to tell him what he meant to her. 'You have stripped his memory of power. You have shown me that there is nothing more potent than love. I'll never be able to thank you enough—'

'Thanks aren't necessary or wanted,' he broke in, his voice rough. 'Will you be happy with the life we'll lead? It will be mainly in New Zealand, because I can't live in Carathia.'

Something in his tone alerted her. 'Why not?' she asked anxiously.

'In the country districts there is a legend that the country will only ever be at peace when the second child in the royal family rules. The rebellion my grandmother fought off was an attempt by her younger sister to take the throne from her. I am the second child.'

She stared at him. 'And this is a problem for your brother?'

'At the moment, yes. The legend has resurfaced, and with it stirrings of rebellion, only my security men have discovered that it's being fomented by a cartel that want to take over the mines.'

'Like Felipe with Moraze,' she said in a low, horrified voice.

'Indeed.' His tone was layered with irony.

Slowly, wondering at the coincidence, she said, 'So you understand.'

'I do indeed. Except that for me there has never been any sense of exile. I have no desire to rule Carathia, and since I was young I've always considered myself more of a New Zealander than a Carathian. I can run our enterprise as easily from New Zealand as Carathia, although there will always be occasions when I have to travel.'

'I'll come with you,' she said quickly. 'But is everything all right for your brother now?'

'Yes, the rebellion has been well and truly squashed.'

'How? Were you—was there fighting?'

'No,' he said calmly. 'I toured the area and told the people that I would never rule Carathia, that I was planning to marry and live for the rest of my life in New Zealand. It seems to have done the trick; once they realised I was in earnest, the agents who were stirring the trouble were greeted with curses.'

She said fiercely, 'It must have been dangerous. Don't you ever dare to do anything like that again.'

He drew her to him, his expression softening. 'You and our children will always come first with me.'

The kiss that followed was intensely sweet. When at last he lifted his head she clung, so filled with joy she couldn't even stammer a word.

He said, 'And once we've said goodbye to Rafiq and Lexie you have my family to meet. You'll like my brother—and he'll like you. Hell, you'll probably even like Rosie's mother, who's as flaky as they come!'

'I can deal with flake,' she told him exuberantly, eyes mischievous in the glamorous witchery of moonlight. 'I'm so happy I can deal with anything. I can't wait to marry you and live with you in your house on the hill overlooking our bay.'

He laughed, drew her into the warm circle of his arms, and kissed her again. Home at last, Hani knew that from now on she would always be safe in Kelt's love.

0909/01a

MILLS & BOON

# MODERN™

## On sale 18th September 2009

### DESERT PRINCE, BRIDE OF INNOCENCE
#### by Lynne Graham

Prince Jasim was convinced that Elinor was a gold-digger and decided to ruthlessly seduce her... But she was a virgin – and is now pregnant with the Prince's baby!

### THE ITALIAN BILLIONAIRE'S SECRETARY MISTRESS
#### by Sharon Kendrick

After a passionate night with her boss Riccardo Castellari, Angie is mortified. She tries to resign, but Riccardo is determined otherwise...!

### HIRED FOR THE BOSS'S BEDROOM
#### by Cathy Williams

Italian tycoon Leonardo hires Heather, who's a mile away from his usual slim sophisticated bedmates. But her inexperience proves the ultimate challenge for Leo...

### MISTRESS TO THE MERCILESS MILLIONAIRE
#### by Abby Green

Kate can have any man she wants – except cold-hearted millionaire Tiarnan Quinn! Yet their nights together begin to reveal a different man beneath the hard exterior...

### PROUD REVENGE, PASSIONATE WEDLOCK
#### by Janette Kenny

Miguel Gutierrez has everything except his wife's love. Miguel is determined to make her regret her callous disregard of their marriage vows...

Available at WHSmith, Tesco, ASDA, Eason and all good bookshops
www.millsandboon.co.uk

0909/01b

MILLS & BOON

# MODERN™

## On sale 2nd October 2009

### *RAFFAELE: TAMING HIS TEMPESTUOUS VIRGIN*
#### *by Sandra Marton*

When Raffaele meets his arranged bride, she's not quite what he was expecting. However, Raffaele knows he'll soon have her purring like a kitten!

### *BRIDE: BOUGHT AND PAID FOR*
#### *by Helen Bianchin*

Romy needs Spaniard Xavier's help. As payment, Xavier demands Romy in his bed again! This time, he'll make sure she stays...

### *THE CHRISTMAS LOVE-CHILD*
#### *by Jenny Lucas*

When Grace learns her innocence was part of a business deal, she flees brokenhearted – and pregnant! But ruthless Prince Maksim *will* have her as his princess...

### *ITALIAN BOSS, PROUD MISS PRIM*
#### *by Susan Stephens*

Perky Katie is worlds apart from her new boss. But at his Tuscan palazzo, Kate witnesses Rigo's homecoming – now he's ready to undo Miss Prim's buttons!

### *THE BUENOS AIRES MARRIAGE DEAL*
#### *by Maggie Cox*

After an affair with Pascual Dominguez, nanny Briana fell pregnant and then fled. She never expected Pascual to reappear – or to demand her as his wife!

Available at WHSmith, Tesco, ASDA, Eason and all good bookshops

www.millsandboon.co.uk

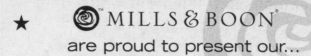

# MILLS & BOON

are proud to present our...

## *Book of the Month*

★ **Expecting Miracle Twins**
by Barbara Hannay ★

Mattie Carey has put her dreams of finding
Mr. Right aside to be her best friend's surrogate.
Then the gorgeous Jake Devlin steps into her life…

Enjoy double the Mills & Boon® Romance
in this great value 2-in-1!

*Expecting Miracle Twins* by Barbara Hannay and
*Claimed: Secret Son* by Marion Lennox

**Available 4th September 2009**

*Tell us what you think about
Expecting Miracle Twins
at millsandboon.co.uk/community*

Fabulous new talent introduced by
international bestseller

# PENNY JORDAN

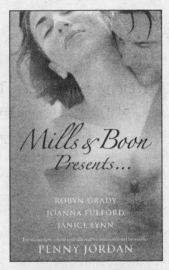

*Three exciting new writers — three
fabulous new novels:*

**BABY BEQUEST**
by Robyn Grady

**THE VIKING'S DEFIANT BRIDE**
by Joanna Fulford

**THE NURSE'S BABY MIRACLE**
by Janice Lynn

## Available 18th September 2009

*www.millsandboon.co.uk*

M&B

# millsandboon.co.uk Community

# Join Us!

The Community is the perfect place to meet and chat to kindred spirits who love books and reading as much as you do, but it's also the place to:

- **Get the inside scoop from authors about their latest books**
- **Learn how to write a romance book with advice from our editors**
- **Help us to continue publishing the best in women's fiction**
- **Share your thoughts on the books we publish**
- **Befriend other users**

**Forums:** Interact with each other as well as authors, editors and a whole host of other users worldwide.

**Blogs:** Every registered community member has their own blog to tell the world what they're up to and what's on their mind.

**Book Challenge:** We're aiming to read 5,000 books and have joined forces with The Reading Agency in our inaugural Book Challenge.

**Profile Page:** Showcase yourself and keep a record of your recent community activity.

**Social Networking:** We've added buttons at the end of every post to share via digg, Facebook, Google, Yahoo, technorati and de.licio.us.

## www.millsandboon.co.uk

VEB/M&B/RTL

™MILLS & BOON®

**www.millsandboon.co.uk**

◎ All the latest titles

◎ Free online reads

◎ Irresistible special offers

*And there's more...*

◎ Missed a book? Buy from our huge discounted backlist

◎ Sign up to our FREE monthly eNewsletter

◎ eBooks available now

◎ More about your favourite authors

◎ Great competitions

*Make sure you visit today!*

**www.millsandboon.co.uk**

# SAVE OVER £60

## Free L'Occitane Gift Set worth OVER £10

As you enjoy reading **Mills & Boon® Modern™** titles we are offering you the chance to sign up for **12 months and SAVE £61.25** – that's a fantastic **40% OFF**.

If you prefer, you can sign up for **6 months and SAVE £19.14** – that's still an impressive **25% OFF**.

When you sign up you will receive 4 BRAND-NEW Modern titles a month priced at just £1.91 each if you opt for a 12-month subscription or £2.39 each if you opt for 6 months. The full price of each book would normally cost you £3.19.

*PLUS, to say thank you, we will send you a FREE L'Occitane Gift Set worth over £10\*.*

**You will also receive many more great benefits, including:**
- **FREE home delivery**
- **EXCLUSIVE Mills & Boon® Book Club™ offers**
- **FREE monthly newsletter**
- **Titles available before they're in the shops**

## Subscribe securely online today and SAVE up to 40% @ www.millsandboon.co.uk

*Gift set has an RRP of £10.50 and includes Verbena Shower Gel 75ml and Soap 110g.*

Offer valid in UK only and is not available to current Mills & Boon Book Club subscribers to this series. We reserve the right to refuse an application and applicants must be aged 18 years or over. As a result of this application, you may receive offers from Harlequin Mills & Boon and other carefully selected companies. If you would prefer not to share in this opportunity please write to The Data Manager, PO Box 676, Richmond, TW9 1WU. For full terms & conditions go online at www.millsandboon.co.uk

Mills & Boon® is a registered trademark owned by Harlequin Mills & Boon Limited. Modern™ is being used as a trademark. The Mills & Boon® Book Club™ is being used as a trademark.

SUB_0909_P9ZEN